True Harvest

Also by Linda Cardillo

Dancing on Sunday Afternoons
True Harvest
Two Mothers: A Saigon Pilgrimage
Across the Table
Love That Moves the Sun
Italian Tales
The Smallest Christmas Tree

First Light Series
The Boat House Café
The Uneven Road
Island Legacy
A Place of Refuge
Catríona's Vow

True Harvest

A Novella

Linda Cardillo

Bellastoria Press

To Stephan,
with thanks especially for
the years we spent in Germany

"The true harvest of my daily life is somewhat as intangible and indescribable as the tints of morning or evening. It is a little star-dust caught, a segment of the rainbow which I have clutched."
                          —Henry David Thoreau, *Walden*

Marielle Hartmann was an only child. This became significant to her only later in life. When she was a little girl, her father, a great bear of a man, would carry her on his shoulders up the dirt road that led to their vineyards. She clutched his hands, giant paws that held her securely as they climbed higher and higher. She could smell the musty, sweet aroma of fermenting grapes that clung to his thick curly hair and she could feel his heart beating steadily beneath her legs. When they reached the top of the hill, he spun her around in a whirling jig and she watched their acres and acres of vines spin with her, their gray-green leaves lifting in the breeze and their fruit pendulous and full of promise.

"Taste this," he said, as he thrust his hand through a tangle of broad leaves and emerged with a perfect cluster of grapes. He held them out to her in his palm, tiny pale globes of translucent green. She felt like a princess then, being offered a treasure of pearls as she surveyed her kingdom.

Behind them the Taunus Mountains formed a barrier against the cold north wind, and below them the Rhine River was a slate blue ribbon warming the soil of their southern-facing slopes. This particular geography had made it possible for her family to grow grapes for over three centuries in a region of Germany that was as far north as Saskatchewan. She understood that only later. As a child, this land was her playground, not her livelihood. It was the earth upon which she learned her father's love.

And as a woman, it was the ground upon which Tomas Marek first stepped into her life.

Chapter 1

October 1975

The clang of Marielle Hartmann's alarm clock ricocheted off the walls of the bedroom that had been hers as a young girl. She reached out from under the down comforter her mother had retrieved from a trunk two days before and turned off the insistent bell. She could see through the slender cracks in the ancient shutters at her windows that it was still dark outside. 4:00 am. Not the banker's hour she was used to waking up to in her high-rise apartment in Frankfurt. Marielle reminded herself that she was no longer in Frankfurt as she looked around the room she had not inhabited in nearly eight years.

She stretched her arms over her head and threw her long legs over the side of the bed and onto the cold stone floor. She could hear her mother already in the kitchen so she grabbed her things and headed to the bathroom. Anita wouldn't be pleased if Marielle were late for the first day of the wine harvest.

Instead of the conservative navy suit she usually wore to her job as an economist at Deutsche Bank, Marielle pulled on a pair of jeans, a flannel shirt and a pair of thick wool socks before joining her mother downstairs.

Anita handed her a mug of coffee and Marielle could see that she had already brewed a full urn to take out to the vineyards for the harvest crew.

"How was Papa's night?" Marielle asked as she sipped the steaming coffee, waiting for the jolt of caffeine she needed to start her day.

Anita shook her head. Marielle could see the fatigue in her mother's eyes, the stoop in her shoulders. She berated herself for not noticing sooner the toll her father's stroke was taking on her mother when she had come to visit in July. Late in the evening during that visit—after her father, Max, had been settled in bed for the night— Marielle had sat with Anita and a bottle of their vineyard's best wine.

Anita had uncorked it with her usual expertise and poured a taste into one of the two golden-stemmed glasses etched with her family's name and crest.

She had set them out on the polished wood of a table in the winery's tasting room. The winery had been in Anita's family for over three hundred years. Anita herself, along with her parents and Max, had brought the vineyards back from the devastation of World War II. In the thirty years since the end of the war she had rescued fallow fields, planting new vines with her own hands, nurturing them through too much rain or not enough, protecting them from disease and finally, reaping the harvest of a unique Riesling that only now was gaining appreciation from wine connoisseurs. Until this spring, Max had been her partner in the enterprise—a man with a nose and a knack for viniculture and winemaking. It was Max who had come to understand and love the land and the grapes it produced.

Marielle remembered trudging through the vineyards as a little girl, racing to keep up with her father as he inspected vines and scooped up handfuls of earth to test its acidity and moisture.

Although Marielle had followed her father around in the vineyards, it was Anita's example that Marielle had absorbed and found fascinating. In the evenings, as she had sat at the dining table doing homework, Anita had shared the workspace with her, managing the difficult decisions about staffing and equipment purchases, setting prices and courting customers. Marielle discovered her talent not only for math in those hours with Anita, but also for negotiating, sometimes helping her to calculate prices and often listening to her bargain with suppliers. When Marielle had scored highly on the *Abitur*, the qualifying exam for university, she was offered a place in economics at the University of Mannheim, one of the best in the country.

With Max and Anita's blessing, Marielle had left home to pursue her studies and create a life for herself in the business world after graduating with honors from Mannheim. Marielle had flourished. At twenty-seven, she was one of only a few female vice presidents at Deutsche Bank. She had spent two years in Hong Kong and had returned only three months ago.

It was while she had been away that Max's grasp of his winemaking and of his world had been obliterated in an instant by a stroke. He was no longer able to walk or to speak, and had made little progress with his rehabilitation. Although she had been shocked by the change in her father and his utter dependence upon Anita, Marielle had been both unable and unwilling to acknowledge what Max's condition meant for all of them—until that evening in July when Anita had poured her the wine.

"Taste it, *Schatz*. Tell me what you think of it."

"It's excellent, Mama. One of the best, I think."

Anita nodded. "Good. At least you can recognize

a good vintage. It's a start." She rubbed her forehead, creased with new lines.

"A start of what?"

"You becoming a vintner."

Marielle sat very still. She had known deep in her heart that her parents—especially her mother—would want her to inherit the winery. But that was decades away. Her second career. Something she had planned after she had made a name for herself in finance.

"Aren't you rushing things a little? You and Papa still have half a lifetime to spend running the business."

"No, Marielle, we don't." Anita's eyes gazed straightforwardly across the table at Marielle. Anita had never been one to tell Marielle fairy tales when she had been a little girl. Storytelling had been Max's role. Anita had been the realist, the practical housekeeper who knew exactly how much food she needed to buy when they opened the winery courtyard in summer for wine tasting dinners; who knew which harvest crews were the best; who had calculated to the penny the cost of producing every bottle of wine.

"We have no time left at all. Papa can't take part in the business. In fact, he can't be left alone anymore. In May, when I was up in the vineyards supervising the pruning, he fell out of bed. I won't put him in a home. But I cannot care for him *and* manage the business."

Marielle stared at her mother, trying to absorb the enormity of what she was saying, trying to deny what she knew her mother was about to ask her.

"I need you *now*, Marielle. Not in twenty or even ten years. I need you to come home. To carry on for me, for us."

Marielle could not answer at first. Her hand gripped the fragile stem of the wine glass with such intensity that it would have shattered if Anita hadn't gently loosened her fingers.

"I know this isn't what you expected for your life right now, to come back to this little village and a life dictated by the seasons after you've been racing across Southeast Asia making deals. But it's not what I expected for mine, either."

Anita sat erect, carrying her responsibilities with uncomplaining acceptance. It was what she had always done. And it was what Marielle knew was expected of her, as well.

And so, in the weeks that followed, Marielle submitted her resignation at the bank and sublet her apartment, wrapping up the loose ends of her life in Frankfurt in time to be here with her mother on this first morning of the harvest.

Chapter 2

Thin wisps of smoke curled from the rusted chimney pipes of the circled campers at the river's edge camping ground. The shadows of bodies stretching and pulling on shirts and sweaters indicated that the men inside the campers were readying themselves for the day.

Marielle steered her mother's ancient Volkswagen bus off the B43 highway that ran along the Rhine where it jogged westward a little north of Mainz. She pulled into the campground and turned off the engine. She considered knocking at the door of Janosch Kosakowski's camper to let the crew chief know she had arrived, but she had no idea which of the ancient metal boxes was his. She decided to wait for the men to emerge and tucked her hands inside her pockets to warm them.

The fog was still thick, hovering just above the water and seeping across the campground, the highway, and then up into the village and the vineyard-covered hillsides above it. The yellow lantern lights within the campers were the only warmth in this gray pre-dawn morning.

Marielle tapped her foot impatiently and watched her breath, wishing she had thought to take a thermos of coffee with her. She pulled her woolen hat down over her ears and blew on her rapidly chilling fingers. She was about to start banging on every camper when the door to the middle one opened and two men stepped out. The first Marielle recognized as Janosch, the Pole who had led the harvest crew for her family's vineyards for the last ten years. Behind him, stooping to clear the doorway, followed a lanky, dark-haired younger man whom Marielle had never seen before.

As if Janosch had given a signal, the doors of the other campers opened and within a few minutes six more men stood stomping in a muddy circle around him. He spoke a few words in Polish, gestured toward the bus and led the others toward Marielle.

She got out of the car as they approached and reached out her hand to Janosch.

"Greetings! Welcome back."

Janosch reached up to pull off his woolen cap and smiled expansively. Marielle's impatience dissipated and she recognized familiar faces. Janosch introduced each member of the crew and they nodded silently or smiled and saluted as he rattled off their names. The last was the tall, man who had shared Janosch's camper. He barely acknowledged Marielle as Janosch announced his name. "Tomas Marek," he said. "Son of my sister."

Marielle opened the VW doors and waved the eight men in, breathing in the aromas of cheap Eastern European cigarettes and fried onions that had saturated the fabric of their jackets. She backed up the bus and headed out of the campground and up to the Hartmann vineyards on the hillside known as Johannisberg—St. John's Mountain. According to legend, it was Charlemagne who had first recognized the potential of this fragment of the Holy Roman Empire and had ordered the first vines planted.

The thing Marielle immediately noticed about Tomas Marek was his hands—pale, slender fingers in a pair of black wool gloves with the tips cut off. They were the hands of a musician—a violinist perhaps— or an artist used to handling delicate brushes. They were hands unmarked by weather or rough work; hands that had not lifted heavy crates of wine bottles; hands that hadn't tilled or planted or pruned. For Marielle, Tomas Marek's hands were both beautiful and useless.

Right now they were hands that he had shoved

into his pockets as he stood on the periphery of the harvest crew while Marielle demonstrated in a mixture of German, limited Polish and gestures what she expected of the crew on this first morning.

She had listened to Anita give these directions for years—to her as a schoolgirl released from the classroom to work the harvest, and later whenever she could spare time from the bank to help her parents bring in the crop. But before she had always been the listener, not the one giving directions. Marielle struggled within herself to set the tone of authority that Anita projected.

"Let them know from the beginning what you expect," Anita had advised. "Hard work, consistent effort, a steady pace, no rotten clusters to augment their baskets. For the most part, they'll work hard. Janosch knows how to put together a good crew—but watch out for newcomers who are either too inexperienced or too lazy to do the job well."

Marielle scanned the somber faces in the misty chill, the men's feet damp and shifting as she spoke. Who among them could she trust to follow instructions, work quickly and competently? Who among them might fail her? They were generally a sturdy group, with knowledge of the task. But her eyes and her doubts kept returning to Tomas Marek, who continued to stand on the edge of the group. He had lit a cigarette and barely listened to her, staring off at nothing since the fog hadn't yet lifted in the valley.

Rather than walk the row as the crew started to pick, Marielle decided to work alongside Tomas for a few hours so that she could gauge his skill. She watched him finish his cigarette and crush it under the sole of his shoe. Like the rest of the crew, he wore a shoddy Eastern European imitation of Adidas sports shoes, and they were already soaked through from the wet grass. Marielle's own feet were still snug in their sturdy Wellingtons, and she remembered hiking Mt. Kenya a few years earlier and being struck by the meager footwear of her guide. He had worn thin-soled leather street shoes yet picked his way nimbly over the soggy, porous lower elevations and later the rocky trail as they approached the summit.

Like the Kenyan guide, Tomas seemed oblivious to the incongruity or discomfort of his shoes. He settled into a crouch and began snipping clusters of Riesling grapes from the lower branches of the vines, reaching behind the curtain of dripping leaves to interior clusters that a less experienced or lazy picker would have ignored. His long fingers deftly cradled a bunch in his left hand and he snapped his shears swiftly and cleanly over the stem. He withdrew his arm from the vine, gently placed the bunch of grapes in the canvas basket at his side, then moved back in for the next cluster. He worked with a steady, graceful rhythm, from the bottom to the top of the stalk, breaking the flow of his movements only to discard a rotten or desiccated bunch.

Marielle had her own rhythm, but she was distracted from it by her own anxiety and curiosity. Watching Tomas, observing not only his skill but also his clearly practiced eye, relieved her concern that he would be an impediment to the harvest. But she could not shake her unease that he was here at all.

The other members of the crew had begun a low, guttural song that rumbled up and down the row. Occasionally Janosch, transporting a full bucket of grapes, would bark an order or point out a missed cluster. Tomas continued silently, filling his basket systematically and only gesturing with his hand when he was ready for it to be emptied. He talked to no one; he did not pick up the song; and he ignored Marielle's gaze, burying himself in the task with an intensity that hovered between concentration and anger.

By ten o'clock the morning sun had finally burned through the fog and Anita arrived with an urn of hot coffee and ham sandwiches. The crew got to their feet and stretched. A few shrugged off jackets and sweaters as the combination of vigorous labor and the heat from the sun began to warm them.

Marielle pulled off her gloves and helped her mother pass out steaming mugs of coffee and the hearty whole grain bread that their neighbor Ute Meyer sold every morning in her bakery. Marielle watched and listened as the gnarled and weathered hands of the crew took their mugs and murmured "thank you." Tomas approached and clasped the thick pottery Marielle held out to him, taking it from her hand with a nod, but barely glancing at her before he turned away.

While the others clustered in small groups, sipping their coffee and munching on their sandwiches with gusto, Tomas walked to the hillside and sat on an overturned bucket. Janosch joined him for a few minutes, leaving an animated discussion with a few of the older men of the crew. He placed his hand on Tomas's shoulder and invited the younger man to join the conversation. But Tomas shrugged and shook his head in refusal.

Marielle heard a sharpness in Janosch's voice but did not understand his Polish. Janosch seemed frustrated with his nephew's withdrawal but didn't waste any more words with him and returned to the group.

Anita had observed the scene, too.

"Is that one going to be a problem?"

"So far he's been surprisingly efficient. Certainly not sociable, but you've always told me we're not up here for a tea party. As long as he continues working the way he did this morning, he can drink his coffee in peace wherever he wants."

"I don't recognize him—Janosch has never brought him before."

"He's Janosch's nephew. He must have worked other harvests before. He definitely knows what he is doing. I can't complain, although I find him perplexing."

"If you have any concerns about him, speak to Janosch. Don't let anything sit unremarked. It will be your undoing as the work gets harder and the crew tires. I've got to get back to Papa. I'll send Ute's son up around 1:30 pm with dinner. The weather's supposed to hold for a few more days, so get as much out of them as you can now."

She put the empty mugs in a basin and climbed in the car, leaving Marielle to call the crew back to the vines for three more hours.

For this round, she left Tomas Marek to his own labors and took up the task of collecting the contents of the buckets from each of the crew. She slipped the straps of a large open canvas knapsack over her shoulders and started at the top of the hillside, working her way down the path between rows of vines, stooping as each man dumped his bucket into her sack. Despite her bankerly life, Marielle had retained the athletic vigor of her student days, when she had been both a long-distance runner and a rower on her university's four-woman boat. During her childhood, Max had been a member of the Rheingau's kayak club and he had taught her to manage a single kayak on the rapidly moving Rhine. Marielle's training and experience had served her and her team well, and she had led them to a German and then a European championship. Although she hadn't rowed on a team since her student days, until Max's stroke she had often strapped a pair of boats on top of the VW and driven off to a local whitewater river with her father on the weekends.

Marielle felt the weight of the grapes on her back and straightened to her full height as she moved down the hill to the wagon with its wide plastic bin. She wanted to demonstrate to the men her ease and familiarity with the work, her strength and stamina. She was used to walking into a boardroom as the only woman and had learned how to be heard, how to be visible to those who would dismiss her. She was determined to be as much of a presence here in the vineyard.

At the end of the day, Marielle reversed her trip of the morning, returning the crew to the campground after a brief side trip to the grocery store so they could pick up provisions for their evening meal. Again, Tomas Marek was silent and reclusive, not joining in the banter and the give-and-take of the other crew members. On the drive back, Marielle glanced into the rear-view mirror and saw him in an unguarded moment—eyes closed, skin sallow, weariness and worry etched into his face.

She bid good night and arranged the pickup time for the next morning with Janosch. Tomas had already closed the door of the camper and lit a lantern as she pulled out of the clearing.

That night, as she soaked in a hot tub, she felt she could enumerate each muscle in her back, her thighs and her calves. She stretched out her fingers in front of her and saw not the smooth, carefully manicured hands that only last week had been tapping away on a calculator. Instead, she saw chipped nails and scratches and felt as if she were coated in a sticky layer of grape juice.

She leaned back in the tub to soak her long hair and then slid momentarily under the warm water, obliterating briefly the images and anxieties of the day.

When she emerged from the bath, muffled in an old sweatshirt and pants she had found in the bottom of her dresser, Anita was waiting with a cup of hot cocoa and a stack of papers.

"How did it go?" She looked straight into Marielle's exhausted eyes.

Marielle nodded. "I got through the day with a decent volume. But I should go down to the tanks and check that Dieter got it all loaded…"

She set down the mug and started for the stairs.

"It's fine. Papa was already asleep, so I went down while you were in the tub."

Marielle smiled gratefully at her mother.

"How did you manage to do all that needs to be done when you were also raising me?"

"I wasn't alone, Schatz."

Chapter 3

Over the next week, the days repeated themselves in a pattern that was as familiar to her as the ancient, meter-thick walls of the winery's courtyard. The too-early alarm clock; the mug of coffee waiting in her mother's outstretched hand; the dense fog hiding the contours of the landscape in the early morning; the groggy and increasingly weary crew stamping their feet in the damp clearing of the campground waiting for their ride. The morning harvest, halting and somber as fingers stiff from the previous day and cold from the near-freezing temperatures clutched at equally cold grapes. The sun eventually burning through the grayness and giving both definition and warmth to the afternoon. The loaded wagon at sunset trundling the harvest down the hill to the tanks. And throughout it all, Tomas Marek's silence.

The rhythm of the days was familiar to Marielle because she had spent every October of her childhood on these hills. She had missed the last two years while she was in Hong Kong, but she hadn't forgotten or lost the knack of progressing along a row of vines, cradling, clipping and dropping grapes into a bucket in one swift, uninterrupted movement. The days were not a challenge to her, especially as the crew got comfortable with her expectations. They treated her with respect, thanks to Janosch.

It was the nights that filled her with anxiety. After returning the crew to the campground every evening and then grabbing some bread and cheese at her mother's insistence, she no longer soaked away the chill and aches of the day in the tub.

She headed instead to the fermentation tanks and her notebooks. She listened to the weather reports, calculated how much was in, how much was still on the vine, and worried about how much time she still had and how high the sugar content of the grapes was from each field.

She stayed late in the tiny office adjacent to the tanks, protecting herself from the cold seeping up from the concrete floor through her feet, up her cramped legs and into her spine by wrapping herself in one of Max's old coats and nursing a fiery glass of

Weinbrand—the limited-edition brandy Max had made every other year. She had driven to the wine school in Geisenheim the week before the harvest began and bought a couple of textbooks on viticulture. It was during these evenings alone that she delved into the books, making notations, trying to absorb what she needed in the only way she knew how—through book learning. Marielle had always been a good student, and she tackled the harvest as if she were preparing for an exam.

But the answers eluded her, as she observed her own grapes not reacting in textbook ways.

One morning as she handed Marielle her coffee, Anita reminded her that she needed to get more rest.

"I saw the light on in the courtyard office at midnight again last night. You're still as stubborn as you were as a child when you couldn't fall asleep until you'd gotten the last piece of a jigsaw puzzle to fit. Schatz, winemaking isn't a puzzle, or even an equation. Sometimes you simply aren't going to be able to solve it."

On the first Sunday of the harvest, Marielle hiked alone to the eastern fields early in the morning to make an assessment of how much was left on the vine. The weather service was predicting an early frost later in the month. Although Max had always reserved a small vineyard close to the house for ice wine—made from grapes picked early in the day, frozen from the first frost—Marielle knew there was still too much hanging to risk harvesting it all as ice wine. She walked up and down the rows, inspecting clusters for mold or, on the contrary, under ripeness. It would do no good to rush the harvest of grapes that weren't ready.

Her head ached from lack of sleep and too many glasses of Weinbrand. With a start, she realized that she had promised her mother that she would accompany her to church that morning. She hadn't been to Mass in years, and Anita herself had not been one to spend much time in the church. But since Max's illness she seemed to have found some peace in the old rituals.

Marielle jogged down the hill, slipped off her boots in the anteroom and ran upstairs to change as her mother emerged from the bedroom.

"You're coming after all?"

"I'll be ready in ten minutes. Who's staying with Papa?"

"Bruno is downstairs in the yard fixing the axle on the wagon. He'll check on Papa for me while we're in church. He does that for me every Sunday."

Marielle quickly washed up, ran a comb through her long hair and put on the navy-blue suit she had worn on the train from Frankfurt when she'd arrived the week before. It already felt stiff and unfamiliar.

Her mother was waiting in the vestibule, handbag

over her wrist. They walked arm in arm down the main street of the village to St. Margarete's, two blocks away, as the bell tolled to announce the next Mass.

Marielle's eyes adjusted to the dimness inside the thick-walled medieval building that had been reconstructed since the bombing of World War II. She hurried with Anita up the aisle and knelt beside her as the priest approached the altar. Remembering the prayers, she followed along, echoing the responses out of respect to her mother, but she felt a great distance between herself and what was unfolding before her. During the homily her mind and her glance wandered, observing the mostly older congregants listening intently to the priest's droning.

Her gaze stopped abruptly, however, when she saw a familiar figure off to the side by the Madonna's altar. Tomas Marek was not listening to the priest, but stood in the shadows, arms folded across his chest, his face illuminated by the flickering light of the candles.

Before Mass was over, Marielle saw him light a candle and then slip out of the church through the side door. He was the last member of the Polish crew she would have expected to see in church, and, in fact, she saw three or four others in the back as she and Anita left. She nodded in greeting to them and they tipped their caps. Later in the afternoon, Marielle went back to the vineyard—not to worry over the crop but to spend an hour sketching. It was her form of escape, to capture with a few strokes of oil pastels the broad sweep of the valley or the detail of a columbine blossom.

That evening, after checking on the tanks and the weather report, Marielle left the winery before eight, intending to finally get some rest before the week began again and the push to finish the harvest intensified.

As she entered the house, she thought she heard a sound that had been an indelible part of her childhood. Max at the piano. He was—had been—an accomplished musician, and had given up a professional career to marry Anita and save the winery after the war. But he had never given up the piano, at least not until his stroke, and had entertained guests throughout the season when the courtyard was open every weekend for wine tastings and festivals.

Marielle was stunned and perplexed by the music drifting down the stairs from her parents' living quarters above the public rooms of the winery. Perhaps Max had made a recording when Marielle had been away. That was the only answer she could imagine as she climbed the stairs. As she got closer, she realized that what she was hearing was the piano itself, not a recording, and for an instant she felt like a child again, wishing that the music she heard meant her father had been restored to her.

When she reached the landing, she quietly slipped into the living room at the end of the room opposite the piano. What she saw was more surprising than if it had been the fulfillment of her wish. Max was indeed sitting in the room in his wheelchair, near but not at the piano. His eyes were closed and his hands lay still in his lap. At the piano, his back to Marielle, was Tomas Marek. His long frame was folded over the keyboard, his head bent into the music.

He improvised as spontaneously as Marielle remembered Max doing on summer evenings, at times plaintive and questioning, and then exuberant and exalting. Max, whose hearing was still acute although he could no longer speak, nodded his head, a smile of childlike joy on his face.

Rather than interrupt, Marielle hung back and retreated to the hallway, listening for a few more minutes before retracing her steps back down the stairs. Reaching into her pocket, she retrieved the ring that held all the keys for the winery and opened the heavy door that led to the business office where Anita kept the files.

Despite her role now in the business and her right to be in the office, Marielle had not yet abandoned the feeling that she was an interloper—an impostor pretending to be Anita, soon to be revealed as a fake.

She tried to convince herself that her concern was legitimate, but she knew she was rifling through the papers not for a management reason but for a personal one.

She wanted to know who Tomas Marek was and why he was here.

In a folder in the middle drawer of the desk she found what she was looking for—copies of the visa applications that Anita had had to file with the government in order to bring the crew to the West. Marielle flipped through the alphabetically arranged pages and found "Marek, Tomas." Amid the stamps and signatures she sought the lines requiring his background. What she read stunned her. Tomas was a surgeon, educated at Jagiellonian University Medical College in Krakow, on leave from the Centralny Szpital Kliniczny (Central Clinical Hospital).

Marielle replaced the papers and returned the folder to the drawer. The music above her had stopped and she heard voices—Anita's in thanks, Tomas's mumbled response, Janosch's more voluble and emphatic conversation.

When she heard their footsteps on the stairs, she remained in the office. She could not explain her discomfort and chose to attribute her reluctance to greet them to her fatigue. Once the outer door closed behind them and Anita had coaxed Max to bed,

Marielle left the office, locked the door behind her and went to bed herself.

Chapter 4

The next morning, still driven by the curiosity that had sent her to Anita's files, Marielle took up a position opposite Tomas on the steep Steinmorgen vineyard. Like all the mornings before this one, a damp chill pervaded the hillside and only the rustle of leaves being parted and the snap of metal clippers separating stems from vines penetrated the stillness. That morning, not even Janosch was humming.

"Your skill is exceptional." she told him. "I haven't often seen anyone except my father handle the grapes as well as you do."

Tomas nodded through the tangle of the leaves to acknowledge that she had spoken to him.

"How did you learn? Have you been at the harvest before?"

"I came as a teenager with my uncle a few times. But we worked for von Hausen then. Later, when Janosch began working for your father, I didn't come anymore."

"Why not?"

"I was studying."

"At medical school?"

Again Tomas nodded, but didn't offer more.

Marielle could see that she was falling behind in filling her bucket and resumed her silence, despite wanting to know what had brought Tomas back to the harvest. She doubted, even if she asked outright, that he would tell her.

Later, when Anita brought a cauldron of lentil soup with ham for the midday meal, she spoke briefly with Marielle.

"Last night when Janosch visited with Papa, I asked him for a favor—to work with you this evening on some of the questions I know you need answered. He's agreed to help."

Marielle started to protest, but Anita went on.

"Janosch has the same *Fingerspitzengefühl*, the same instincts, as Papa, Schatz. You're not going to find everything you need in textbooks. I've seen you night after night, hunched over the desk in the outer office, filling your notebook with numbers. That's only part of what you need to learn. Let Janosch help you. Don't be stubborn. You don't have that luxury. *We* don't have that luxury."

Marielle acquiesced, but only because she did not have any other solution to the knot that had been tightening in her stomach with each passing day. Her fears for the success of the year's vintage grew more intense, especially after all the frustrating nights of trying to grasp what she needed and having the answers elude her. She was reluctant to admit her weakness to the one individual—Janosch—whose respect was vital to the completion of the harvest.

If Janosch thought she was incompetent, his opinion might spill over to the others and she would lose control. Considering Anita's advice about establishing herself as the leader, Marielle questioned why her mother would expose her vulnerability.

She helped Anita repack the station wagon with the remains of the meal in silence and turned back to the grapes for the rest of the afternoon without speaking to Janosch, whose eyes she avoided as she vigorously attacked a row. She worked for an hour before hoisting a collection bag on her shoulders and taking the measure of each crew member's performance as she gathered what they had harvested since the meal. At least she could manage and even master the physical part of the harvest, she thought to herself, if not the critical decisions that she knew she had to make over the next few weeks.

At the end of the day Anita had arranged for a neighbor to drive the crew back to the campground so Janosch could stay to advise Marielle. In the small public dining room that the winery used for tastings and light meals over the winter Anita had left a supper of bread, cold cuts and cheese, and a bottle of the previous year's vintage.

Marielle went to the outer office to get her notebooks before joining Janosch in the dining room. When she returned she was surprised to see Tomas with his uncle. Her already tenuous hold on authority was disintegrating before her eyes if both Janosch and Tomas were aware of her ignorance.

She slid ungraciously into the booth, barely greeting the two men.

Janosch gestured to his nephew and spoke in halting German. "To translate, I ask him to come."

Marielle was impatient to begin and be done, desperate for the help but angry that she needed it.

The men shifted on their feet, awaiting some signal from Marielle. It finally dawned on her that they were as tired and hungry as she was and she pointed to the food.

"Please sit and eat, then we can work."

Marielle could barely swallow and took only small bites of bread and goat cheese while Tomas and Janosch filled their plates and savored each mouthful of the simple meal. Marielle remembered her role as host and uncorked the wine, pouring three glasses. The bottle was from the Steinmorgen acreage, the same fields they had picked that day.

Marielle knew that without looking at the label. Max had taught her as a girl that each of their patchwork of fields—both contiguous as well as scattered, and each with its own name—produced distinctively flavored wines. All of their grapes were Riesling, but the composition and acidity of the soil, the drainage, the angle of the sun all affected the quality and taste of the different wines. She remembered what a discovery it had been to her, to the child she had been then, and how Max had made a game of it, masking the labels and having her guess with her nose whether she was tasting a Marcobrunn or a Steinmorgen or a Johannisberg. She had loved to accompany him on the Feast of the Ascension, when he had led a group of guests on a hike throughout their vineyards. At each field a trestle table had been set up with tasting glasses and wine made from the grapes grown in that soil the previous year. At the end of the hike, at the top of the northernmost field, Anita was waiting with vintner's stew and cucumber salad and crusty bread to soak up the sauce. Often there had been forty or fifty guests, sunburned, sated, enjoying the view of the valley as they sat at the outdoor feast.

Marielle said a silent prayer to the memory of those days and hoped that she would have the wines to serve next spring when she would lead the hike herself for the first time.

Reminded of why she was sitting here with Janosch, she opened her notebook as he wiped the crumbs from his lips.

"Shall we begin?" she said, reining in her anxiety.

For the next two hours, Janosch spoke to her through Tomas, trying to convey in words what he sensed through his fingertips and his nose. He tried to articulate what for him was as instinctive as breathing. Marielle kept seeking specifics— measurements, temperature, chemical analysis. But Janosch had no notebooks, no records like a chemist in a lab. He tapped his head and his heart.

"It's all in here. I watched and learned from my father. He taught me how to recognize when the grapes are ready to be picked, when the fermentation has reached its optimum.

"Max knew these things. If you had been at his side you would know them as well, instead of searching through the pages of a book."

Marielle felt her face redden; her humiliation intensified by Tomas's presence. Although she had followed her father around as a little girl, she had abandoned his side once her studies began. From the time she was fourteen she had propelled herself through school, preparing for the university qualifying exam—the *Abitur*—long before her classmates had begun to apply themselves to learning. When Desiree Schultz, the daughter of a neighboring vintner, had been elected queen of the wine festival the year she and Marielle were eighteen, Marielle had ignored the entire festival in order to study. Hadn't that paid off for her? She had won a place in economics at a prestigious university, graduated with honors, been hired immediately by Deutsche Bank, the only woman to secure a position.

To prove herself in that environment, Marielle had continued to do what she knew best. She worked long hours at her desk, running regression analyses, pouring over columns of numbers and pages of graphs, always prepared at meetings where she was the only person in a skirt at the table. She had been relentless with herself in learning as much as she could and had earned respect for her diligence and intelligence. It had not been easy, but it had been familiar territory for her, concepts she knew she could grasp. The challenge of proving herself to a phalanx of skeptical men in suits had not been fraught with terror, as the task before her now was.

She looked at the two men sitting across from her at a table whose scratches and patina she knew intimately. Their drab and ill-fitting Eastern European clothing, their slumped and weary postures and their unshaven faces were a sharp contrast to the bankers in their tailored suits, Italian shoes and Swiss watches who had wanted data and projections and ample bottom lines from her only a few weeks ago. But Marielle was intimidated by these men, resistant to what Janosch was trying to teach her and frustrated that he could not articulate to her what she needed in a way she could understand. It was not merely the gulf between his Polish and her German, but the distance between a man of the earth and a woman of the mind.

At ten in the evening, the second bottle of wine emptied, Marielle closed the notebook, finally giving in to everyone's fatigue and the knowledge that the next day's dawn would be upon them far too soon. She offered to drive them to the campground but Tomas told her that Anita had offered them two old bikes that had been sitting unused in the shed. They would pedal back.

When they left, Marielle cleared the plates and washed up in the winery's café kitchen; the sound of the running water hid her tears.

The next morning in the vineyard Tomas approached her during the break. She was startled to have him initiate a conversation with her. She saw the dark circles under his eyes and regretted how late she had kept him the night before.

"I'm sorry for the late hour yesterday evening. I'm

sure when Janosch said yes to my mother he wasn't anticipating how much help I needed."

"It's not the time that my uncle regretted as much as his inability to teach you. Or rather, in his words, your inability to learn."

The briefest smile skimmed across Tomas's face; the first time Marielle had seen any emotion at all. She was stung by Janosch's criticism but felt that Tomas was attempting to make like of it.

"He's an old man, set in his ways, who has little use for the science of winemaking. He believes that too much science will destroy the unique character of each wine—create a dull uniformity that relies on duplicating a formula over and over instead of experimenting and trusting one's instincts with the chance of developing a wine with true brilliance."

"And what do you believe?"

"I'm somewhere in the middle. I have great respect for my uncle and know his frustration with the factory mentality of the Party's approach to winemaking in Poland. But I *am* a scientist. In the same way that I rely upon both my training and my instincts when I encounter a problem during surgery, I know that one needs both to produce a successful vintage."

"So, you disagree with your uncle?"

"To a certain extent. For example, I don't think you are unteachable." Again, the flicker of a smile.

"It sounds as if Janosch has given up on me."

"But I haven't. I have an offer to make you. I know enough about the science and the art that I think I can show you what you need to learn, in a way you will understand. Will you allow me to help on my own? Not as a translator of Polish, but as a translator of the intangible?"

"Why would you?"

"Because my uncle is a friend of your father and does not want to disappoint him. And because my uncle's reputation is his livelihood, so a failed harvest will reflect badly on him. There are many families in Poland who are dependent upon Janosch's ability to bring the crew to this vineyard year after year. What we are able to earn here in one season we cannot make in a whole year in Poland. Not even I, as a physician. I know you have wondered about what would bring someone like me to work the harvest. You have no idea, here in the West, how little our economy can support. I'm not the only one on the crew who is an educated professional. Thadeusz is a civil engineer. Matthias is a teacher of mathematics. But they cannot feed their families—I cannot feed mine—without the work here in your vineyards. If you fail, many people will suffer."

Marielle stood with her arms folded across her chest listening and absorbing Tomas's message. Her burdens were increasing as if she were carrying a heavily laden basket of grapes on her shoulders. She shifted her weight and straightened her back, not willing to be daunted by the magnitude of the responsibility.

"What are you proposing?"

"I'll stay behind in the evenings as we did last night and work with you. I can't promise you success, but I can give you the tools you'll need to make success possible. The rest is up to you, the weather, the market."

Marielle felt herself stiffen as her terror surfaced again—in broad daylight on the hillside instead of in the darkness and solitude of night.

Tomas saw the expression on her face and felt a brief stab of compassion for her struggle to fill her father's shoes.

"There will always be risk. Always elements you can't control. I can't give you predictability and certainty, if that is what you're looking for."

Marielle shook her head. She had learned with Max's stroke that life was not predictable and certain. She understood intellectually that, even with as much science as she could get her hands on, she would still face obstacles. But in the past, she had always been able to rely on herself, find the resources within to solve her problems. She hated having to trust someone else.

Tomas, taking her silence and stiffness as a refusal, shrugged and turned away with bitterness.

"Fine, suit yourself. Find your own answers."

"Wait."

Marielle unclasped her tightly entwined arms and reached out to touch him on the shoulder. He stopped, but didn't turn around.

"I accept your offer. Please stay this evening."

He nodded brusquely. "Bring the harvest records for the last ten years. Perhaps we can identify some patterns."

And he walked away, pulling his gloves out of his pockets as he took up a position on the row where he had left off.

That evening, after driving the rest of the crew back to the campground, Marielle prepared a platter of Parma ham, cheese and pickles and carried it out to the fermentation room where Tomas was making notations. They ate quickly and silently before spreading the records of the last decade across a worktable. Heads bent, they studied the numbers, pointing out exceptions or oddities, marginal notes of weather aberrations, anything that could give them clues to the success or failure of a vintage.

They worked till nine. Marielle would have persisted, pushed herself to stay longer, but she felt guilty about keeping Tomas late the night before and knew she had to balance her need for him now with the work she knew awaited them the next day in the vineyard.

"You should go, get some rest."

"So should you. You can't make good decisions if you are sleep-deprived."

"Yes, doctor."

She gathered up the paperwork and turned off the lights as Tomas pulled his bicycle from the shed. Although he was still an enigma to her, Marielle felt a sense of reassurance as she watched him pedal away toward the river. She shut the gate to the courtyard and closed the latch. Wrapping her sweater around her, she climbed the stairs to her room. Despite her agreement to get some rest, she did not sleep right away but studied her notes. She found no answers yet, but knew she had made a beginning.

For the remainder of the harvest she met with Tomas nearly every night, listening, absorbing, struggling to assimilate what he had to impart. One evening he asked her to characterize each of the last ten years' vintages—to describe them not with data but with words, images.

"I don't even remember some of them. I wasn't here during many of those years."

"How can you be a vintner if you don't know your own history? It's one of my frustrations with the Party in Poland—they're trying to create a new society without memory. You can't abandon responsibility for what came before simply because you were sitting at a desk in Frankfurt. That's not who you are anymore."

"These lessons are supposed to be about winemaking, not about who I am or am not." Marielle spoke to him as she would have to a subordinate, not a colleague.

"Very well. If you can't remember then I suggest we retrieve bottles from each of the vintages and start tasting."

They trudged down to the wine cellar and began filling a crate with the long-necked brown bottles that were standard for the region. When the crate was full Marielle insisted on carrying it to the dumbwaiter and hoisting the rope that sent the load to the upper level.

In silence she set out a basket of crackers and a tray full of tasting glasses etched with her mother's seal. Then she began uncorking bottles.

Her fury at being lectured by Tomas masked the fear she felt at having no definable identity. He was right that she was no longer a banker. But she had nothing to replace that role, nothing that was hers. To Janosch and the crew she was merely the daughter of the chief, not the chief herself. She assumed that Tomas also saw her as unformed, amorphous, filling the shape of whatever vessel was presented to her: the hardy field worker, shouldering as much weight as the men; or the dilettante vintner, acting the role but not truly embracing it. His accusation had stung so sharply because she felt so adrift, so unsuited for the title "vintner." If she weren't a banker anymore—and she wasn't—or a vintner, who was she?

When she finished uncorking all the bottles she started with the oldest and poured them a taste of 0.1 liter from every year and every vineyard. She picked up the first glass, looked Tomas in the eye and raised it slightly in a mock toast.

"To your experiment."

With each glass she made notations, searching for words to describe each of the wines. Tomas drank with her. At first, Marielle was deliberately sullen, recording her impressions only in writing and not sharing them with Tomas. To her surprise, he didn't object.

"This isn't an exam, you know. I'm not the teacher waiting for you to recite back my lectures. You're your own teacher here." And he raised his glass containing the 1969 Marcobrunn Spätlese.

Tomas's remark released some of the pressure she always felt to perform well at every task. As she proceeded deeper into the neat rows of glasses she had arrayed on the table, she began to make discoveries—subtle differences, echoes, textures. Max had taught her to appreciate and enjoy wine, but this evening with Tomas began to reveal a complexity and beauty that ten years' worth of data had not. It also made her drunk. Even though they took only a sip from each glass, there were nevertheless many of them. Her reserve, the way she normally presented herself, began to dissolve. At one point she exclaimed over the quality of a wine she had just sipped and launched into a verbal description that reopened the conversation with Tomas. As she tasted and noted the year on the bottle, she pulled out of her memory anecdotes of particular experiences when she had worked the harvest.

"The weather was so warm that year—not at all like now. I remember wearing a yellow t-shirt and shorts and the sweat dripping down my back."

"That was the year the Auslese won a gold medal. I came home for the dinner to congratulate my father. I was sitting next to him when one of his colleagues asked what he had done differently that year and he answered that winemaking was like jazz. Improvisational. Inspired by the moment, by the energy of those around him, by the emotions churning within. By the willingness to shift tempo or key and head off in a new direction."

As she spoke the memories became less about the wine and more about her relationship with Max.

"You're very close to your father, aren't you?" Tomas asked.

"Yes. Are your parents still alive? Healthy?"

"My mother is. She lives with us in Warsaw, works as a bookkeeper. My father died before I was born. My older sister, although she was only four, remembers the day when my mother, pregnant with me, learned of his death."

"I'm sorry—for her, and for you that you never knew your father."

"Janosch has been a father to me. My mother turned to him, her brother, and he stepped in. It's because of him that I went to university and studied medicine. I was an angry boy in my teens. I wanted to be a musician."

"But you *are* a musician!"

He lifted his eyebrows to question how she knew that. Marielle felt her face redden.

"You were listening the other night?"

"Sound travels in the house. I couldn't help overhearing you. You were good. And you made my father happy, for which I'm most grateful."

"So you were watching, as well."

"I didn't want to intrude. My father's face was so blissful. If I had said anything, I would have broken your spell."

"I hope my daughter grows to love me as much as you love Max."

"Your daughter? How old is she? Is she with your wife while you are here?"

"Magdalena is seven. My wife is gone and

Magdalena lives with me and my mother and our old nanny who cared for my sister and me while my mother worked. Now she cares for Magdalena. I miss her. She doesn't understand when I am away for so long. I worry that when I go back, she will turn away from me for abandoning her."

"Don't worry. Speaking as a daughter, I can assure you she will forgive you."

The glasses were empty. The notebook was full. It was 1 a.m.

"I should help you wash up before I head back to the campground." He rose and began to place the glasses on the tray.

"I'm concerned about you cycling back at this late hour, and I've had too much wine to drive you back. Why don't you sleep here? I can make a bed for you on the couch in the office."

"No, it's too much trouble. I'll be careful."

"It's no trouble at all. If you *don't* stay, I will worry all night about your safety. Would you start the washing up while I can get the bedding?"

Marielle left before he could protest again and tiptoed up to her room to retrieve pillows and a duvet from her trunk. By the time she had made up a bed for him he was placing the last glass on the drying rack.

She handed him a towel and a bar of soap and pointed out the bathroom.

"I'll have a mug of coffee waiting for you in the kitchen at 5 am. Sleep well. And thank you."

Tomas watched as she turned and walked up the stairs, notebook tucked under her arm. It had been a long time since he had revealed so much of himself. He wasn't sure if it had been the wine or the vulnerable young woman whose memories had released his own.

Chapter 5

A few days later, Marielle experienced a far different form of Tomas's help. A rainstorm rose quickly in the vineyard late in the afternoon, an isolated squall that came with little warning, black clouds looming over the mountains carrying a disastrous cargo of water and wind. Because their backs were turned away from the mountains and the sky across the river to the south was still a luminous blue, the harvest crew didn't sense the storm till it was upon them. Huge drops of rain fell first, splattering across heads and hands, shaking the broad leaves, sending the birds on the hillside into scattered flight.

Normally, rain didn't deter the pickers. Although uncomfortable, they continued on, sometimes at a slower pace as shears became slippery or visibility blurred. But Janosch, emptying a load of grapes into the wagon, saw the ominous blackness descending and yelled in warning to Marielle and the rest of the crew. A bolt of lightning arced down into the trees above them. He threw a canvas tarp over the wagon and secured it with rope just as the deluge began.

Marielle called the others away from the vines and most of them withdrew to huddle under the long flaps of the canvas. Tadeusz, on the eastern side of the row, motioned that he would finish his side, with only a few meters to go, Marielle nodded an okay.

She watched in dismay as the rain pelted the fragile fruit, unsure how much of it would withstand the downpour. The rain was so heavy that it had already cut into the alleys between the rows, forming streams of mud and stones that poured down the hillside.

Suddenly, a swath of churning water came rushing toward them from above, bringing with it the debris of the hillside to the north—broken vines, rocks the size of a man's head, a pair of rusted and forgotten shears, a glove.

"The creek that runs across the field must have overrun its banks," Janosch shouted to her over the din of the hammering rain.

Their location, huddled around the wagon, placed them just beyond the reach of the rising water that was gathering momentum as it raced down the hillside. Except for Tadeusz, who couldn't hear their shouts and didn't see the water until it was at his knees.

The others watched in horror as the water lifted him, carrying him away as if he were a leaf and not a 150-pound man. He grabbed hold of a branch but the force of the water was so strong that it ripped the whole vine out of the earth with its root intact and swept them both farther down the hillside. Marielle saw the fear in Tadeusz's eyes as the water turned him on his back and he disappeared over the next drop in the hill.

Tomas and Matthias bolted from the shelter of the wagon, parallel to the destructive channel formed by the roiling water. They found Tadeusz unconscious, his body halted by an outcropping of rock. They managed to pull him away from the rising water to soggy but safer ground. Marielle, her fears for her grapes now replaced by concern for Tadeusz, ran to meet them.

Tomas was bent over Tadeusz's limp body, breathing into his mouth, then beginning chest compressions. He worked silently and confidently, undeterred by the blood streaming from Tadeusz's forehead where he'd been battered by the rocks.

Marielle stood back with Matthias, sheets of rain drenching her, as Tomas continued. When he saw her, he asked her to protect Tadeusz's head from the rain. She stripped off her waterproof anorak and held it over him, keeping the water away from his face. Tomas worked tirelessly, his movements purposeful and focused, alternating between compressions and breathing.

Finally, Tadeusz coughed, his chest heaving, and Tomas rolled him onto his side as muddy water was expelled from his mouth. With Tadeusz breathing on his own, Tomas carefully checked him for bruises. It was then that he and Marielle saw the oddly twisted orientation of his left leg.

"The impact of being thrown against the rock must have broken it," he said. He shouted to Matthias, "Can you find me something to use as a splint?"

Matthias returned with a discarded post that looked long enough and strong enough for Tomas's purpose. Marielle took the cotton scarf from around her neck and tore it into strips. At Tomas's direction, she held Tadeusz's head in her lap.

"Hold him down if you can. This is going to be excruciatingly painful for him."

With deft, sure hands, Tomas aligned the broken leg and bound it to the splint.

"That should prevent further damage until we can get him off the hillside."

The rain continued unabated. Marielle was

reluctant to risk another life by sending someone down to the lower ground to obtain help and decided to wait out the storm. From her vantage point, she could see that the village square had been flooded by the overflowing creek. Flashes from fire engines and rescue vehicles indicated that the danger and destruction had not been confined to the vineyards.

Marielle and Tomas were soaked to the skin. Tomas had removed his coat to cover Tadeusz to conserve his body temperature. He held Tadeusz's hand, occasionally checking his pulse, and spoke to him in calming tones. Marielle stroked his head, which she still supported in her lap. Although the color had drained from his face and it was creased in pain, he was conscious and breathing.

Tomas looked across at Marielle and nodded.

"Thank you," he said.

"Thank *you*. You saved his life."

As the rain finally subsided, Marielle saw headlights climbing the hill and realized it was Anita in the station wagon. She brought with her the news that two people had drowned, trapped in a basement apartment. A pregnant woman and her little girl had been swept through the village in their Volkswagen, but had managed to escape when the car collided with a streetlight in the square.

After Anita's arrival, they improvised a stretcher and carried Tadeusz to the car. Tomas rode with him to the hospital in Eltville, and Marielle turned to her rain-soaked, debris-strewn land. She sent the crew down with the wagon to the winery when she could see that the water below had receded, but stayed on the hillside by herself to assess how much she had lost.

She trekked across the fields, counting up the damaged rows, holding back her fear. The destruction was limited to the single field where they had been working that afternoon, a result of the path taken by the unleashed creek. Although the crew would need to spend a day or two at the end of the harvest in clean up, most of the grapes still on the vine had been spared. She was grateful for that, but more grateful for the life spared that afternoon and for Tomas's presence on the hillside—and in her life.

Chapter 6

After the storm, Marielle's confidence grew as she tackled the remaining days of the harvest. The yield promised to be higher than she anticipated. The weather held and only the small acreage near the house was left when the first frost settled on the valley. The crew had the vines picked clean before the sun began to warm the earth—perfect conditions for ice wine. Although she still had much ahead of her before the success of the vintage would be apparent, Marielle no longer felt out of control or terrorized by what she didn't know.

The morning of November 11 dawned crisp and clear. It was *Martinstag*, the feast of St. Martin. The winery planned to open its doors that evening for a small celebration after the traditional parade and bonfire in the village. Around four in the afternoon, just before sunset, Joseph Krechel, one of the tallest men in the village and a fireman, donned the costume of a Roman centurion, complete with plumed helmet, polished breastplate and red cape. He mounted Ralf Schmid's white stallion, whose bridle was decorated as lavishly as Joseph himself, and horse and rider arrived in the square in front of the church. A hundred children from the kindergarten and the elementary school waited impatiently with their parents, decorated lanterns hanging from long sticks swinging restlessly in their small hands. As soon as Joseph took his place at the head of the line the firemen's band brought their horns to their lips and began to play. Parents lit the lanterns and the procession moved forward, the horse prancing and the children singing about the unselfish St. Martin, who cut his cloak into two pieces and gave one to a freezing beggar.

All along the route of the procession townspeople watched, some joining in the singing and walking along with the children. By darkness they had arrived at an open field at the edge of the village where the fire brigade had built a towering pile of scrap wood and roped it off. The children formed a circle around the wood. Joseph dismounted, removed his red cloak and draped it over Gregor Sperling, who had played the beggar with great gusto every year since he had graduated from high school. Then Joseph took a torch from a waiting colleague and lit the wood.

To the excitement of the children, the fire rose quickly through the towering pile. Ute Meyer began moving around the outer circle, distributing her large, doughy pretzels encrusted with salt crystals.

Marielle had not attended the St. Martin's Fire since she had left the village. It wasn't a tradition that adapted well to a dense urban environment like Frankfurt. She had walked down to the field with the procession when it had passed by the winery and she stood now, pulling apart one of Ute's pretzels as the flames crackled and shot into the air.

Tomas had been leaving Gruber's Appliance Store where he had spent some of his harvest earnings on a toaster and a Bosch coffeemaker for his mother. He saw the bobbing lanterns of the children turn the corner at the end of the square and felt a pang for Magdalena. She had made a lantern for today as well, decorated with leaf rubbings, his mother had written him in her last letter. He decided to follow the procession for a short distance, sharing in his daughter's experience a thousand kilometers away.

When he got to the bonfire, he saw Marielle across the clearing and watched her face in the firelight. He saw both exhaustion and tenacity reflected in her expression. Her hair fell in loose waves around her shoulders instead of in the severe braid she had worn throughout the harvest. He had considered her attractive before, but in a conventional way. Tonight, however, watching her in an unguarded moment, singing with the children, he was touched by her vulnerability and openness. She looked beautiful to him. An unexpected wave of tenderness washed over him as he stood on the periphery of the circle. Her circle. Her life. Not his, he reminded himself, and turned away with his shopping bags.

The next morning, their campers stowed with Miele washing machines and other West German goods purchased with some of the Deutsch Marks they had earned, the Polish crew made ready to depart from the campground. As Tomas and Janosch made final preparations, Marielle pulled into the clearing and jumped out of the car. She had two packages in her arms and breathlessly approached the two men.

"I was worried that you had already left," she murmured. "I had these for you last night, but you didn't come by." She tried not to sound plaintive, but her voice was tinged with disappointment and internally she winced at her own neediness.

"I wanted to say thank you, to both of you."

She handed Janosch the larger bundle. "My mother told me of your fondness for hazelnuts. I hope you enjoy this."

To Tomas she held out a flat package about the size of a book.

"On Sundays I did some painting. I've noticed how you gazed out over the valley during breaks and I thought you might like this small memento."

Tomas unwrapped the package and held up a watercolor of the scene that had surrounded him for the last six weeks.

"Thank you." He took Marielle's hand and shook it. "Goodbye. My best wishes to your parents."

Marielle stood in the middle of the campground as the crew formed a caravan and headed out onto the highway. She stared after the gray ribbon of ancient vehicles until it was out of sight.

Chapter 7

On January 5 Max died in his sleep. He had enjoyed the Christmas holidays with Anita and Marielle and had watched the fireworks on New Year's Eve from the upstairs parlor windows that looked out over the river. It had been too cold to take him to the top of the hillside where he and Marielle had always watched when she had been a girl.

Anita came to wake Marielle. She was still in her robe and slippers and Marielle knew immediately something had happened. It was unlike Anita not to be dressed for the day well before Marielle ventured from her bed.

"What's wrong?" she asked her mother as Anita gently called her name.

"Papa is gone." And she took Marielle in her arms.

After the funeral Marielle helped Anita to sort and answer the condolences that had flooded into the winery as news of Max's death had spread. In the stack of envelopes that had not yet been opened she found one with a Polish stamp, addressed to her. She reacted with a sharp physical pain in her chest as if she'd been startled by a loud noise in the middle of the night. She put the envelope aside to open later in the privacy of her room.

The paper was a thin, cheaply made sheet the color of dirty dishwater and the words had been formed with a ballpoint pen that skipped occasionally. But as she read the words, she saw Tomas's long fingers moving across the page and heard his voice as if they were sitting in the winery late at night. His letter was tender and thoughtful, remembering how much Marielle had loved Max and calling to mind the images she had described the night she drank too much.

"You hold much of your father within yourself. Don't forget that as you mourn him, because he lives on in you. He was a fortunate man to have a daughter like you, Marielle, and I know he loved you."

For the first time since the morning Max died Marielle cried, trying not to spill her tears on the fragile paper for fear it would disintegrate. That Tomas understood her loss and the special nature of her connection to her father touched her deeply. His empathy spoke to what Marielle believed must be his relationship to his own daughter. But it took her breath away that he understood the guilt she felt in not being the natural vintner Max had been. Throughout the fall she had berated herself for not paying more attention when she had been younger, for not being present for so much of her adult life. When she had left home for university and the wider world, she wondered if Max had ever regretted her going or felt that she had turned her back on him. She questioned if Max had even been aware that she had taken on his responsibilities in those last months.

As these thoughts overwhelmed her, her body was engulfed in sobs—both for her father and for the man in Warsaw who was offering her hope and forgiveness.

The next morning, she woke at dawn to Tomas's letter on her night table and sat in her nightgown at her desk to answer him. She expressed her gratitude for his understanding and for the kindness he had shown Max during the harvest. She reminded him of the joy she had seen on Max's face the night Tomas had played the piano for him. She didn't trust herself to write of the depth of her own feelings when she had read Tomas's note. She didn't reveal to him how deeply he had touched her and how much he had seen into her soul.

Later that morning she added her letter to the stack of acknowledgments she had written for Anita and took them to the post office. And then she waited, not conscious that she was keeping track in her mind of the days it would take for the post to reach Warsaw, be delivered and read by Tomas, allow him to respond and then for the response to travel back to her. That she was waiting for a reply seemed foolish to her—ridiculous to want something so unattainable. He had probably written merely out of courtesy and by accident had found the words that spoke so directly to her. He had no intention, she was sure, of continuing the correspondence. When two weeks had passed without a reply, she acknowledged that her expectations had indeed been unrealistic, and she was relieved that she had been restrained in her reply to him.

She tried to put him out of her mind.

She threw herself into the winter rhythm of the winery—preparations for the bottling of the harvest, calls to customers confirming their orders, plans to schedule the concerts and performances that took place every summer in the courtyard, equipment maintenance that needed to be done. She was in the office on the morning of February 14 when she heard the doorbell. Anita had gone to do the marketing so Marielle answered the door. Maria Marangoudakis, a Greek immigrant who ran the florist shop in the railroad station, stood on the stoop with an elaborately wrapped bouquet.

"It's for you Marielle—not a late funeral arrangement. The request came by wire from Warsaw."

She handed over the flowers with a twinkle in her eye and climbed back onto her bicycle. The attached cart was filled with more flowers destined for others in the village who would soon be smiling as broadly as Marielle.

Marielle took the bouquet into the winery kitchen to find a vase large enough for the dozen long-stemmed roses that she discovered under the layers of cellophane and yards of ribbon. The roses were a deep burgundy with petals like velvet. Tucked deep in the center of the bouquet was an envelope with her name on it, scrawled in Maria's hand. But inside the envelope was the printed copy of the wire itself, with the order for the roses and the text of the message. Her hand trembled as she unfolded the yellow sheet of paper and read what it held.

Dear Marielle,

Happy Valentine's Day! Although such frivolities are discouraged, I thought that a gift of flowers for you alone (and not simply in memory of your dear father) would be a way to brighten what has been a dark winter for you. Your note reminded me of the many hours I spent at your side during the harvest and how much I miss your curiosity and drive and tenacity. I have framed the painting you gave me and it hangs in my office at the clinic—a constant reminder of the woman who painted it and what she sees every day. It links me to you. Forgive me if the roses are inappropriate—a gift that should come from a lover rather than a friend. I thought of making up some excuse about florists only having roses today, but the truth is, I asked for roses.

Yours,
Tomas

Marielle read the note over and over, her eyes leaping from one phrase to the next. Were these the words of a friend, or of one who wished to be more than a friend? Why had he chosen St. Valentine's Day to send the flowers if he only intended a gesture of friendship? Why was she feeling such turmoil? She wanted with all her heart to simply enjoy the lush and lavish burst of color and not agonize over its meaning. She was shocked by how quickly her perception of Tomas had changed when he had written her after Max's death and understood her so clearly. Had she been denying to herself her own feelings toward him? Had those feelings only been allowed to blossom after he had left and no longer was a man whom she employed—a man who was a thousand kilometers away? Marielle didn't know what to do with her feelings.

She brought the vase into the office and placed it on her desk, where its emphatic presence filled her sight and she could inhale its rich scent.

When Anita returned, she stopped in the office and saw the bouquet.

"Who are these from?"

"Tomas Marek."

Anita looked at Marielle with curiosity.

Marielle shrugged. She wasn't ready to admit her wonder at what was happening between her and Tomas.

"A belated condolence," she explained. "I'll send him a thank you note."

That evening Marielle struggled with her feelings and her response. She was surprised by her longing for Tomas, a longing that had been muffled through the winter by the strain of Max's deteriorating condition and death. She had been so preoccupied with the impending loss of her father that she had not recognized her sense of loss after Tomas's departure. She had been lonely during the winter, but she thought it had been because she had left friends and colleagues behind in Frankfurt. Her life, now dictated by the demands of the land, the seasons, no longer intersected with lives driven by urban commerce. Even though Frankfurt was only 50 kilometers from the Rheingau, it had become increasingly rare for her friends to come to visit. Evenings spent laughing over a glass of wine as a release from the pressures of business were no longer a part of her life. But she realized that she didn't miss those evenings at all. She realized that what she missed were Tomas Marek's hands—gesturing in the dim light of the fermentation room as he explained a concept, or cradling a cluster of grapes in the autumn sunshine, or brushing against hers as he gathered up the papers strewn across her desk.

She tried to imagine him in Warsaw, composing his note to her late in the evening after he had returned home from the clinic and spent an hour reading to Magdalena before putting her to bed. She saw his hands again, gently moving a strand of Magdalena's hair away from her face as she slept, pulling the comforter up around her shoulders to ward off the chill in the poorly heated apartment. She saw his hands loving and protecting, and longed for them to love and protect her.

The longing was impossible to fulfill. It stilled her own hands, and she found she could not write to him at all.

The next morning, she sent a brief wire assuring him that the flowers had arrived, that they were beautiful and that she was deeply moved by his words and his gift. She didn't want to appear ungrateful for what had been an extraordinary expense for him. She was overwhelmed, in fact, by the extravagance of what he had done and said. But she held in check her hope that the longing she felt was shared by him.

She spent the day impatient and irritable, thrusting crates of empty bottles out of her way when two days before she had stacked them in the courtyard exactly where she had wanted them. She broke the pen she was using to fill out some order forms when she pressed too hard, splattering ink across the page and onto her shirt. In the kitchen at midday, she slammed cupboard doors and tore open a package of noodles, spilling most of them on the floor.

Anita, as if dealing with an unruly toddler, said nothing and retrieved her dustpan and whisk broom from the closet and began sweeping up.

"I'm sorry, Mama. Let me clean up the mess."

"It's nothing, almost done. Why don't you put the water on to boil and I'll finish."

"I can't seem to do anything right today. Everything, even the slightest inconvenience, is annoying me."

"When you were younger, you used to act like this when you had to make a choice about something and were afraid."

"Afraid?"

"Afraid of taking a risk. When you were learning

to walk, you couldn't quite bring yourself to let go and take a step. But it made you so angry that you would throw your toys. You wanted so much to go, but a part of you always held back. Cautious. Tentative. Your frustration was so palpable. Like it is now."

Marielle looked at her mother.

"What is holding you back, Schatz? Are you afraid he doesn't love you as much as you love him? We never truly know another's feelings. It's like the leap of faith you had to take this fall with the vintage. Trust your instincts, even when you don't have all the data. And believe me, any other woman who received a bouquet like you did yesterday would consider that all the data she needed."

"How did you know?"

"I knew before he left here in November. You may not have recognized it in yourselves, but when the two of you were together you radiated. I saw him watching you when you weren't aware of it. He couldn't take his eyes off you."

"It's hopeless, of course. That's why I'm so paralyzed. He's in Warsaw. I'm here. If I let myself love him—open up the Pandora's Box of my emotions—we are only setting ourselves up for heartache and disappointment."

"If you ask me, the Pandora's Box has already been opened, and if you try to stuff your feelings back in you will just face more days like today filled with anger and frustration.

"Your father and I were separated for years during the war. Months went by with no word from him. But our love survived. You'll find a way."

"What should I do?"

"I can't tell you that, Marielle. But you will know. Be still and listen—to yourself and to him."

The next day, her answer came in the form of another wire from Tomas.

"Come to Warsaw for Easter," it said.

And she did.

Chapter 8

April 1976

Her bags were filled with gifts. A doll and picture books for Magdalena; stockings and well-made gloves for Tomas's mother, Halina; handkerchiefs and a merino wool shawl for Nyanya, the nurse who had cared for Tomas as a child and now looked after Magdalena; and food for the Easter meal—ham and oranges and cheese and fresh peas. She also brought some of Anita's plum preserves and cookies that she had baked herself the night before she left and packed between layers of waxed paper in a tin.

The train ride was long and complicated, across West Germany, into Czechoslovakia through Prague and then north into Poland. At border crossings in the middle of the night she woke to the insistent knocking of guards on her compartment door. Flashlights flicked from her papers to her face and the chilling sense that she could be denied entry or worse if she answered the gruff, rude questioning of the border guards incorrectly.

Exhausted, she arrived in Warsaw two days after her departure from Frankfurt. She washed her face in the lavatory with the trickle of water that was left, re-braided her hair and put on some lipstick as the train pulled into the Central Station. She made her way down the platform seeking Tomas's familiar face but seeing only strangers.

At the end of the platform, she put her bags down and waited. There was a grayness to the building and the faces surrounding her. Soldiers with Kalishnikov rifles slung over their shoulders patrolled the main concourse. In contrast to the hectic pace of the Frankfurt station, travelers moved more slowly and there were far fewer than she had expected to see. There were one or two food stalls selling sausages and one aqua blue cart offering orange juice mixed with seltzer served by a kerchief-bedecked older woman who rinsed out her glasses in a dishpan filled with murky water and then reused them. A newsstand was the only other sign of commerce. There was no florist or restaurant. The space was cavernous, but remarkably empty.

She was startled when she felt a hand on her shoulder.

"I'm sorry I'm late," she murmured as she turned toward him.

She took in his gaze, his dark eyes ringed by circles of fatigue, his skin no longer showing the effects of six weeks in the open autumn air but reflecting the same gray-tinged pallor she had seen on others in the station. She reached up to touch the face that she had been imagining for weeks as his hands encircled her shoulders and he bent to kiss her.

At first, he offered her the platonic continental greeting of a kiss on each cheek. But the proximity of their bodies, the sensation of his cheek against her skin and the memory of his scent as he leaned in toward her caused her to move closer into the circle of his arms. The tension of the long journey began to loosen and her body softened, molding itself to the contours of Tomas's angular frame.

He was thinner than she remembered as he pulled her even closer, wrapping his arms tightly around her. His lips moved from her cheek to her mouth and she felt as if he were breathing life into her, not only reviving her after the exhausting journey, but also filling her up after the emptiness and loss of the winter.

He did not stop kissing her. After her mouth, he

kissed her eyes, her neck, her fingertips. A smile lit her face and he laughed out loud.

"I can't believe you are here and in my arms."

"I can't believe it either. I don't recognize myself right now. I feel like a madwoman or an addict."

He lifted her. She felt the strength in his arms and placed herself in his care, allowing him to carry not only her body but her spirit.

"My mother and Magdalena are waiting at the apartment. I'll have to let you go long enough for them to satisfy their curiosity."

He gathered her suitcases and led her to the street and the trolley.

She sat by the window and at his urging looked out at the city instead of at him. He held her hand, his long fingers entwined with hers, gently stroking as if to convince them both that their presence together was real, confirmed by the evidence of touch, skin, pulse.

They changed trolleys twice before arriving at his apartment block on the outskirts of the city. There was no elevator and he carried her bags up the narrow staircase to the sixth floor. Vestiges of cabbage and onion permeated the stairwell. They passed others descending the stairs and Marielle was aware of the blatant glances sweeping over her from her head to her shoes. Everything about her looks and her clothing screamed "Western economy." She had noted as she watched from the tram that even the young women were dressed drably in shapeless clothing. She had never considered herself overly concerned with style, but her well-made skirt and sweater and especially her shoes had drawn excessive attention.

She wondered if she would be causing Tomas difficulty as so obviously a Western woman.

When they arrived at the landing she stopped worrying about the impact of her clothing. She could hear the chatter of a young girl, querulous and insistent, behind one of the doors, and a much older voice answering her.

Tomas placed his key in the lock.

"Papa!"

Marielle stepped back as Magdalena leaped into his arms. She peeked over Tomas's shoulder at Marielle and stared at her, then whispered into Tomas's ear. He whirled around with Magdalena still in his arms and welcomed Marielle into the cramped hallway of the apartment. Standing at the end of the hall by the kitchen was an older woman, her head shrouded in a cotton scarf, her house dress covered in an apron, her back bent with years of physical work. She nodded at Marielle but did not smile when Tomas introduced her as Nyanya.

Magdalena continued to demand her father's attention, pulling at his shirt and babbling away in a staccato-paced recitation. They moved down the hall together and to a door on the left that led to the living room. Two sofa beds lined the walls and a dining table and chairs filled the opposite end of the room by a lace-curtained window that looked out over the city. In the distance, Marielle could see the looming tower of the Palace of Culture. At the table sat a tall woman in her fifties, who despite her simple skirt and blouse, had an elegant bearing. Her dark hair, with no sign of gray, was pulled back into a French knot.

She rose and stretched out her hand to Marielle.

"I am Halina Marek, mother of Tomas, sister of Janosch, who tells me many things of your family and your vineyards," she said in German. "My sympathy at the loss of your father. Janosch had great respect and love for him."

Marielle took her hand and returned the firm grasp, knowing that Halina, while gracious, was measuring her. Marielle had no doubt that Halina, like her own mother, had recognized the depth of Tomas's feelings. She was acutely conscious of her position as an intruder in this house full of women—all of whom had their own special connection to Tomas. She wondered if he was equally aware, or oblivious to the impact of her presence here.

She glanced around the cramped space and wondered if she and Tomas would find the privacy to explore further the physical closeness they had tasted at the Central Station. Perhaps she should have insisted on booking a hotel when he had first suggested that she come. She hadn't wanted to impose on their hospitality; now she felt even more the disruption that her visit was causing.

But her concerns were postponed by the noisy bustling of Nyanya, who marched into the room with a steaming soup tureen.

"*Zupa!*" she declared, depositing the bowl firmly on the table and gesturing for everyone to sit.

After the meal, Marielle distributed her gifts. Magdalena became absorbed in dressing and undressing the doll; Halina expressed appreciation for her thoughtfulness and Nyanya clucked over the shawl but was more thrilled with the food. She told Marielle through Tomas that she would now be able to prepare a feast with what Marielle had brought.

Marielle offered to help her, a gesture that was noted but refused by the old woman. She did allow Marielle to carry the packages into the kitchen and Marielle then understood that it was Nyanya's domain. The narrow room had barely enough space for one person to work. In one corner was a bed that had been the old woman's since she had arrived from the countryside thirty years before to care for the infant Tomas. Under the bed were all her worldly possessions, stored in salvaged cardboard boxes and fastened with saved string.

Tomas and Marielle spent the afternoon in the park with Magdalena, who persisted in her reluctance to talk to Marielle. When prompted, she had whispered a barely audible *"Dziekuję"* for the gifts earlier in the day. Marielle waited on a bench and watched as Tomas pushed Magdalena on the swings and caught her as she slid countless times down the slide. She took pleasure in observing Tomas with his daughter. His affection for her, expressed in small gestures of tenderness, caught in Marielle's throat. She thought of his hands earlier that day, grazing her softly as he led her out of the station, caressing her on the tram, lifting her firmly to bring her level with his eyes and his longing. She had no idea when or how she would feel his hands in such intimacy again. She knew she wanted that—and more. She also knew that the devotion she was witnessing between Tomas and Magdalena, a devotion she understood to her core, closed off even the glimmer of hope she had that she and Tomas might have a future together. Tomas would never leave Magdalena. And the regime would never allow Magdalena to leave Poland with Tomas.

Marielle bit her lip and forced back the tears that were too close to the surface. She would not mar the three days she had on her visa by wallowing in what was denied to her. She got up from the bench and found a piece of chalk by the edge of the playground's asphalt surface. Kneeling, she sketched out the boxes for hopscotch and then searched the bare ground for a flat stone.

Curious, Magdalena watched her. Marielle offered the stone to her but she shook her head and hid behind Tomas. Tomas took the stone instead and tossed it on the first square. He began hopping, much to the amusement of both Magdalena and Marielle. When he missed, he handed the stone to Magdalena and she began to play. But when her turn was over, she handed the stone back to Tomas.

"*Nie!*" He shook his head and pointed to Marielle. "It's Marielle's turn!"

Marielle held her breath, half expecting the girl to throw the stone on the ground and stalk away. But something in her father's tone clearly warned her that was not acceptable. She reluctantly held the stone out to Marielle, and Marielle smiled at her.

"*Dziekuję.*"

The girl turned to her father. "She speaks Polish?"

"She's trying. Maybe you can teach her."

They finished the game, with Magdalena pointing to each of the numbered squares and repeating their names for Marielle, who stumbled through their pronunciation.

On the walk back to the apartment they counted in sing-song, Magdalena riding on Tomas's shoulders.

After supper that evening Tomas explained the sleeping arrangements. Marielle was to have the single bedroom, normally occupied by Halina and Magdalena. They would sleep on the sofa beds in the living room and Tomas planned to sleep at a neighbor's on the floor below. Marielle, dismayed at the disruption, insisted on sleeping on the sofa and allowing Halina and Magdalena to stay in their bedroom. Despite much protesting and insistence, it was finally settled when it became clear that the little girl needed her own bed to fall asleep. After she was settled, Janosch joined them and Halina brought out a bottle of vodka and four narrow glasses.

"It's not Riesling, but it's our national drink," she said, as they toasted to the friendship between the two families.

Around midnight Janosch took his leave and Halina said goodnight. Nyanya had long before closed the kitchen door, muttered her prayers and turned out the light.

Tomas smiled at Marielle.

"You've survived your first day."

"Are you surprised?"

"No. I expected you to charm all of them. And though you may not believe it or realize it, you have."

He took a step toward her and pulled her to him. She felt the warmth of his breath on her neck, the security of his arms around her, the press of his lean body against her own. He kissed her slowly, so many times that she lost count, and once again she found herself melting into him, the rigidity with which she had contained herself throughout the day giving way to a softness and a willingness that was new to her. She had never known herself to be so pliant. She felt him slip his arm under her and carry her to the bed. For an instant he left her there and she was bereft, thinking he was leaving. But he had moved away only to turn off the light. The immediate darkness was total. No streetlights burned outside the apartment to cast even a hazy illumination through the window and there was no moon. She felt him before he was close enough to see the outline of his face. He stretched his body the length of hers and pulled the duvet up over them. Despite the April date, temperatures still dropped at night and they had turned off the heater hours before to conserve fuel. Warmth spread over her from his closeness and her own surging blood. He began to kiss her again in silence, and then moved his hands down across her body.

Marielle wasn't without experience with men. She'd had a steady boyfriend at university and had stumbled through the awkward couplings that had come at the end of long hours of studying or Saturday evening gatherings where too much alcohol had been consumed. After graduation they had drifted apart, especially when Marielle had gotten the prestigious offer from Deutsche Bank. For a while she had dated another expatriate while she was living in Hong Kong. But neither relationship had prepared her for the emotional intensity of her feelings for Tomas. She felt as if every nerve ending in her skin was alive; every brain cell was firing in joy. Every part of her body—muscle, skin, blood—was attuned to this moment and Tomas's presence and nearness. Although she had been conscious moments before of Nyanya's snoring behind the kitchen door and her ears had been alert for the sound of Magdalena waking from a dream, now she heard nothing but Tomas's steady breathing and his heart, beating beneath her hand on his chest.

They made love in silence, with at first only the gentle escape of a sigh as, freed from the layers of clothing and restraint they had carried all day, their skin first made contact—belly to belly, legs wrapped around each other, arms taking each other in. In the past, Marielle had often felt as if she were outside her body when she'd had sex, watching herself go through the motions, responding to touch, following the lead of her partner, but never fully engaged. For the first time in her life, Marielle was no longer an observer, but lost in the midst of a deep pleasure that seemed to obliterate the distance she had always kept between herself and others. She was surprised by how emboldened she was, how hungry for Tomas and his body. She pulled him into her, wrapping herself tightly around him, aware of her power as she felt him respond to her with a hunger as aching and desperate as her own.

She didn't know herself as she felt the boundaries between her body and his dissolve, ignoring the geographic and political boundaries that had dominated her thoughts in the weeks leading up to this night. Their lovemaking allowed her to forget, if only for these few hours, what separated them. Surrounded by the dark nothingness that disguised the limits of Tomas's life, she let those limits slip away—the bleak apartment block; the cramped flat crowded not just with furniture and belongings but also with the unfulfilled needs of the three people who loved Tomas so intently; the constant sense of struggle to meet even the most basic necessities of life. For a blissful few hours, the darkness and the silence gave Marielle and Tomas only each other, because that was all they could perceive. Heartbeat, breath, lips, hands were their only reality.

They fell asleep briefly, their bodies slick with sweat beneath the comforter despite the chill in the room. At 3:00 a.m. they woke and made love again, but with a more bittersweet mood. He murmured that Nyanya would be awake soon and he would have to at least make the pretense of having slept on his neighbor's sofa. He drew away, kissing her lips and then her forehead and then her now tangled hair as he rose from the bed. He pulled on his pants and sweater and eased himself out the door of the apartment.

Marielle rolled over to where Tomas had lain, breathed in his familiar scent and hugged herself as she tried to close her eyes to the approaching dawn and the encroachments of Tomas's life.

Morning began early in the Marek household. It was Easter Sunday. Nyanya was up at five to begin the preparations for the meal. By six, Magdalena was chattering to her grandmother and soon after, Marielle could hear through the thin walls the sound of drawers opening. She thought about remaining under the covers longer but sensed that Magdalena would soon be out of the bedroom. She feared that whatever tentative steps Magdalena had taken toward her yesterday would be obliterated in an instant if Magdalena came bounding over to the bed normally occupied by Tomas and found Marielle instead.

She threw back the comforter and forced herself up, taking the bathrobe she hadn't used the night before out of her suitcase and slipping it on just as Magdalena opened the bedroom door. Marielle, toothbrush in hand, was on her way to the bathroom as Magdalena scanned the room.

"Where's my Papa?" she asked Marielle in Polish.

Although she understood the question, Marielle's

grasp of the language wasn't enough to answer.

From the bedroom, Halina answered her granddaughter.

"He spent the night with Anton—don't you remember he told you when he kissed you goodnight? He'll be back soon and we'll all go to church. Come here now and I'll braid your hair."

"Not yet, Babula. Breakfast first," and she ran to the kitchen.

Marielle washed up quickly in the bathroom, cautious of the limited water supply, and dressed in the living room while Magdalena ate in the kitchen with Nyanya. She brushed the tangles out of her hair, braided it and then wrapped the braids around her head. She hadn't worn her hair like this since she'd been a little girl but something about the day and her sense of being pulled back in time by Warsaw drew her hands into the familiar pattern of plaiting.

She made the bed and stored the pillows and linens in the storage compartment under the mattress. Smoothing down the skirt of her suit, she went into the kitchen.

It was warm with the steam rising from boiling potatoes. Cucumbers, peeled and sliced paper thin, were draining in a colander over the sink. A bowl of pastry dough covered with a kitchen towel was rising at the back of the stove. Nyanya gestured to the pot of coffee on the burner and got up to cut her a slice of bread. She held out an egg as well, but Marielle replied with a "No, thank you."

Magdalena stared at Marielle as she poured herself a cup of the thick coffee in the pot.

The little girl asked her something, but Marielle didn't understand her.

"Nie rozumiem." I don't understand.

Magdalena jumped out of her seat and tugged at Marielle to stoop down to her level. When she did, she touched the braids circling Marielle's head.

"Who?"

Marielle pointed to herself. "I did."

Magdalena then ran from the room, calling to Halina. In a minute she was back with her hairbrush and bobby pins and thrust them into Marielle's hands. With an elaborate pantomime, she demonstrated that she wanted Marielle to braid her hair the same way.

When Nyanya realized what was going on she shooed them out of the kitchen.

"No hair in here!" she scolded.

Marielle took her coffee and moved into the living room with Magdalena and sat beside her on the sofa. She was surprised that the little girl wanted her attention, but she threw herself into the task, brushing out the tangles gently and then coaxing the wispy strands into neat braids. It was the first time she'd had such tactile contact with a child. With no siblings, she hadn't had the opportunity to be "Auntie" to anyone, and she had grown distant from the women she'd gone to high school with who now had children. It was comforting to have Magdalena so near, to smell her soapy fragrance and to have her so clearly enjoying the work of Marielle's hands.

When she finished, she dug a compact out of her purse, opened it up and put the mirror in Magdalena's hands so that she could see the braids. Magdalena touched the side of her head and beamed.

At that moment Tomas entered the apartment. He was brought to a standstill by the sight of Marielle and Magdalena side by side with the same hairstyle — Marielle's a deep chestnut and Magdalena's golden.

"Good morning, my ladies," he said, his eyes lingering on Marielle as the color rose in her cheeks. She wasn't sure how she would get through the day when she felt a sense of memory sweep over her body as Tomas took all of her in with his eyes.

"Papa, look at my hair! Just like Janina and Kasia." She twirled around.

"You look like a very grown up young lady. Grandma must be very happy that you sat still long enough for her to braid it."

"Grandma didn't do it! *She* did."

"Marielle? Did you thank her for such a beautiful job?" Halina had come into the room and touched Magdalena's braids. She had in her hands a circle of brightly colored artificial flowers decorated with blue ribbons.

"*Dziekuję*," murmured Magdalena.

"Would you like to wear the flowers to church?"

Halina set the flowers on her head and Magdalena fidgeted with them till they fit comfortably.

"Now you look like a proper Polish young lady."

Together, the whole family, including Nyanya in her black dress, walked to church, Magdalena's ribbons bobbing as she hurried to keep pace with the adults. The service was long and Marielle was fascinated by the devotion of the congregants. Unlike in Germany, the church was filled not only with old women. Young families, couples, groups spanning generations like the Mareks, crowded the pews and spilled into the side aisles. It was a revelation to Marielle that the church was so viable here. Although she didn't understand a word of the sermon, she recognized the passion of the priest in the pulpit and watched the rapt faces around her, nodding as he spoke. She watched Tomas as well, tracing with her eyes the planes of his face and body that she had caressed the night before with her hands.

After church, Marielle helped Halina set the table while Nyanya finished the meal and Tomas and Magdalena played a game of checkers in the bedroom.

"He has so little time with her, he must make the

most of the weekends," Halina confided. "It's never enough for her. She's afraid of losing him the way she lost her mother."

It was the first mention of Tomas's wife. Marielle was torn between wanting to know and wanting to deny her existence. In the end, she decided that she needed to know.

"How?" she asked.

"She left one day for work and didn't come back. Magdalena was four—old enough to question, to believe somehow that it was her fault. My daughter-in-law was a troubled young woman and she suffered mentally. Tomas searched for her for many months, forgetting himself, forgetting his child, blaming himself for something he couldn't fix."

"Did he find her?" Marielle realized she wanted the answer to be yes; wanted Tomas to have that emptiness behind him; wanted him to be free to love *her*.

"He did. She was destroying herself with drugs. She'd been a nurse and so had easy access to painkillers, which she had started to take to kill the pain in her spirit. In the end, they killed her as well. Tomas brought her home, got her help, but it wasn't enough. She overdosed—about a year ago now. Thank God, not here, not in front of her child. They found her under a bridge on the outskirts of Ujazdowski Park."

Marielle was very still. The suffering of this family and their ability to put one foot in front of the other and continue on was incredible.

"I'm so sorry, Halina. Thank you for telling me. It explains so much."

"I wouldn't have told you, wouldn't have betrayed my son's privacy, if I hadn't witnessed what has passed between you in this short time. Tomas does not know how to protect himself in love. He suffered greatly with the loss of Krystyna. I can't bear to have him suffer again. I want you to understand that before you go any deeper into this relationship. He will not abandon his child."

"I know that, Halina. I will never ask that of him."

"Then, unless you abandon your mother and your vineyards, I don't understand what you two are doing to each other."

"I don't understand it either. But I've never loved anyone the way I love Tomas."

"Then God help you both."

Chapter 9

At two in the afternoon, Janosch arrived with his wife, their daughter and her husband and their two daughters, Janina and Kasia, whose hairstyle Magdalena had been delighted to emulate. The family crowded around the table and ate and drank, including the newly bottled wine Marielle had brought from the 1975 harvest—a wine that would soon be described as "phenomenal" by experts. The meal stretched out over several hours, with vigorous discussions punctuating the gaps between the courses. Nyanya clucked over everyone and smiled with satisfaction at the feast she had produced with the gifts Marielle had carried across the border and her own bartering and haggling. Tomas had told Marielle how Nyanya would head out of the apartment in the morning with an empty net bag and some treasure she could trade. She traveled across the city on three trolleys to the bazaar and negotiated and cajoled at open stalls for black market meat and fruits that were not to be had with ration coupons at the government stores. Somehow she had always managed to feed them, even when shortages and soaring prices had put even the most basic necessities out of reach. Her pride at this Easter meal was palpable, and the family was rewarding her with the highest praise—their vociferous enjoyment of everything she put on the table. Pierogi stuffed with potatoes and cheese, wild mushroom soup, ham, potatoes baked with eggs and sour cream, stuffed cabbage, and for dessert, pastry twists and cheesecake.

It was past eleven when the last of the pastries had been eaten, the vodka bottle was empty and the three little girls had fallen asleep on the sofa. Janosch and his son-in-law each carried one of the cousins down to the car. Halina carefully slipped Magdalena's dirndl off and tucked her into bed while Marielle and Tomas cleared the remnants from the table.

By midnight Nyanya had turned off the light in the kitchen and closed the door. Halina bid them goodnight, but with a penetrating glance at Marielle that Tomas didn't miss.

"What was that look for?"

"She's a mother who loves her son and doesn't want to see him hurt."

"Does she think you are going to hurt me?"

"She thinks we are hurting each other—that it is madness to continue when we cannot be together."

"Is that what you believe."

"I did in the beginning. No, wait. I still think it's madness. But I can't stop loving you. It's too late."

"It's too late for me as well."

He took her in his arms. Their lovemaking that night had an elegiac quality to it, a consciousness that this touch, that kiss, would be the last for many months. Marielle wanted to commit to memory the sound of his voice whispering her name, the hollows of his body into which her curves fit, the scents of both of them mingled on his skin. She clung to him afterward, unable to sleep or to let him go until it was nearly dawn.

In the morning, Marielle said goodbye to the three women. Nyanya blessed her and put a small packet of herbs in her hand.

"For the *zupa*," she directed.

Magdalena kissed her on the cheek and stepped back. Halina embraced her silently.

With Tomas, she reversed her trip of Saturday morning, traveling by trolley to the city center and the train station. Tomas had arranged with the clinic to have the morning off so that he could spend these last few hours with her. They sat in silence in the stuffy trolley, a light rain spattering the windows. He held her hand.

"Thank you for coming. It was a lot to ask."

"Thank you for asking. There was nowhere else I wanted to be." She hesitated, then asked the question that was hovering between them.

"Will you come for the harvest?"

"Yes."

She nodded. They rode in silence again until the transfer point, where they changed lines.

"Is this what our lives will be from now on? A few days of bliss each year punctuating a lonely existence?"

"I won't ask you to do that. I've been lonely for a long time, even before my wife's death. I'm used to it. My time with you is a gift. But you—you have a world of opportunity before you. The vineyards, your friends. Your life is full of possibilities. Don't close yourself off to those possibilities because of me."

She turned to him.

"There is no other possibility for me except you."

A look of both pain and hope skimmed across Tomas's face as she spoke.

"It's too much to ask of you," he protested.

"It's too much to ask me to let you go. I don't know what else to do except wait for the harvest and store up from our time together what will sustain us for the rest of the year."

She kissed him as the trolley pulled into the station—a firm, determined, decisive kiss. There was no more to say. No other solution.

They parted on the platform as the final boarding call for the train to Prague was announced. He held her firmly against him. He buried his face in the scent of her hair, still in its braids. She leaned into his chest, pressing her ear one last time to the steady rhythm of his heart.

Once on the train, she took a window seat on the side of the platform and watched for as long as he was visible. He remained on the platform until the last car had made the bend beyond the station. Then he turned and walked back into his life.

Chapter 10

1976-1982

Tomas and Janosch and the crew returned in the fall for the harvest. Marielle had renovated an unused wing of the winery in the ell over the tank room, turning it into an apartment for herself. It was there that she intended to live with Tomas for the six weeks of the harvest. She anticipated Anita's objection. The village was small; opinions of the Polish workers among the older members of the community were often negative. Even though the entrance to the apartment was within the enclosed courtyard and not on the street, Marielle knew it wouldn't be long before the gossips began chattering over loaves of bread at Ute's bakery.

She braced herself for the conversation with her mother as they painted the new rooms in late August.

"Mama, I want you to know my intentions when Tomas arrives in October. I'm going to invite him to stay here instead of at the campground."

"That's gracious of you to wait to move in until after the harvest. Why not ask Janosch as well? I'm sure he'd appreciate not having to live in that cramped tin box."

"Mama, this is difficult for me to explain. I mean to invite Tomas to stay *with me* in the apartment."

Anita put down the paintbrush and looked at her daughter.

"Do you realize what you are exposing yourself to? Not only the criticism of the village, but a weakening of your position with the crew! You're the chief; they are the workers. To be so blatant about your relationship with Tomas is damaging to your authority. It's suicidal."

"Mama, this whole relationship is suicidal. I can't live with him; I can't live without him. At least for these few short weeks, I intend to give us the life we can never have!"

"It's a pretense. A fairy tale. You cannot flaunt it. I'm not telling you to stop loving him. Believe me, I understand. But don't live with him while he is here. This isn't the anonymity of Frankfurt. You'll suffer in subtle ways because of the judgment of others. Listen to me, Marielle."

Reluctantly, Marielle acquiesced to Anita's advice. She asked Tomas and Janosch to stay in the apartment and gave up her fantasy of a few weeks of domestic life. But the apartment connected via an internal door to the main part of the house and both Anita and Janosch ignored Tomas's nightly visit to Marielle's bedroom.

They deepened their intimacy during those nights—sometimes simply falling asleep in each other's arms, physically exhausted by the day's labor. Sometimes they continued conversations that had begun earlier in the evening, about the vineyards, about Magdalena and, as the end of the harvest approached, about their relationship.

Tomas continued to struggle with his belief that he was cutting Marielle off from the chance to live a full life—with a husband and a family.

"I'm not sure I ever saw that as the direction my life would take—especially when I set out on my career at Deutsche Bank. Now that I am responsible for the winery, my life is full. The vineyards are my children. I'm not missing something in my life because of you. On the contrary, you're filling an emptiness that had been there for a long time.

"Tomas, I'm not going to deny that there is nothing I want more than to be your wife. But that isn't within my reach. Perhaps we *can't* make this work. But I'm as committed to you as if I wore your ring."

Tomas left that year as he had in the past, on the morning after St. Martin's Day. They watched the flames of the bonfire together, his arm lightly around her waist, grateful for these last moments together and the ritual of the fire, warming them as the darkness and the winter of separation closed in on them.

Tomas returned for two more harvests without another visit by Marielle to Warsaw. Anita finally relented the third time and no longer cautioned Marielle about the propriety of his living with her during the harvest. She had witnessed the constancy between them during their annual separations—letters weekly and always, on Valentine's Day, a huge bouquet of roses, delivered first thing in the morning by Maria.

When Karol Wojtyla, the archbishop of Kraków, was elected as Pope John Paul II in 1978, a new energy and sense of identity surged in Poland. In 1979, Marielle returned to Poland at the same time as the Pope. When he knelt on the tarmac at the airport and kissed the ground of his homeland, Marielle understood the emotional meaning of this visit and acknowledged her own connection to Poland. As it did for John Paul II, a piece of her heart remained on Polish soil, even though her life's work and responsibilities lay elsewhere.

With thousands of other people, but conscious only of the man by her side, Marielle experienced one of the Pope's outdoor Masses and began to grasp what she had observed at the church on Easter Sunday a few years before. For Poles, the Church was more than devotion and prayer. It was the constant that defined them despite a turbulent history of shifting borders and foreign oppression. With this second visit, Marielle fit another piece into the puzzle of understanding Tomas.

During the months of separation between harvests, Marielle accumulated more puzzle pieces in the form of Tomas's letters. They were a journal, recounting the minutiae of his life in a way that allowed Marielle to imagine his daily existence. As she moved through her own life, pruning, planting, rushing to the hillside after a particularly devastating storm to survey the damage to the vines, she would sometimes pause and see him—treating patients at the clinic, seated at the dining table with Halina and Magdalena in the evening, attending a recital when Magdalena began studying the violin. It was reassuring to her to know that he was living in a world parallel to her.

As the date of the harvest approached, however, she would develop a heightened emotional state. Despite the letters, she always felt a stab of uncertainty. Each year was as if they were beginning anew, with an initial reserve that marked the first day of his arrival. Tomas and Janosch always came to dinner the first night, a meal Marielle prepared with great care. She drove into Wiesbaden to the food market in the lower level of the Carsch-Haus department store and selected meat and produce from the abundant displays at each stall. One year she made duck roasted with apples, raisins and sauerkraut that had been braised in Riesling. Another time she chose a leg of lamb that she simmered with onions and bacon in a sauce made from broth and Burgundy and served with dumplings.

In some ways, the elaborate preparations for the meal and the ritual of the meal itself were a way to ease the transition from life without Tomas to Tomas as a daily presence. She poured her energy into chopping and peeling and stirring to still the voices in her head, the questions about how Tomas would react to her when he walked through the door.

Each time he arrived, he greeted Anita first—in the early years with a simple handshake and later with a kiss on each cheek that she warmly returned. Then he took Marielle in his arms and bent to kiss her, holding her with his eyes closed for a moment as they both relished the reunion.

Their first night together always began tentatively, an exploration of achingly familiar territory. But as their bodies eased into each other their hesitancy gave way to a recklessness and abandon and outpouring of all that had been pent up during their months of separation.

For seven years these reunions repeated themselves, deepening and sustaining their love for one another. Marielle's wines were gaining attention as she grew in confidence and knowledge in her winemaking; Magdalena turned thirteen during Solidarity's revolutionary impact on Poland and was developing into a bright and motivated student. Tomas was named head of surgery at the hospital.

Chapter 11

1983-1988

In the spring of 1983, Marielle came face-to-face with the consequences of the choice she had made to lead this divided and often incomplete life. The Rheingau Vintners' Association arranged a trip for the group to travel to the Mosel region to visit the vineyards of a similar group of vintners. Marielle, at Anita's encouragement, decided to go. It was a valuable opportunity to learn new techniques and be exposed to new ideas. It was also more fun than Marielle had had in a long time.

She realized how narrow her world had become in the years since she had taken over the winery. She had devoted herself to the business and had only made time for Tomas—writing to him every week. Her friends from Frankfurt had long since moved on in their lives—furthering their own careers at the bank, starting families. Relaxing for a few days with colleagues who shared the same challenges was a delightful respite. She laughed, hiked through glorious countryside and sat over lingering meals with a different wine for each course.

She also met a man. Klaus Eckhardt ran a winery in Kiedrich, about twenty kilometers north of her village. He was about forty, an outgoing and energetic man who reminded her in many ways of her father. There was an earthiness and frankness to him—a man without pretense who considered himself first and foremost a farmer. He sat next to her on the bus and entertained her with hilarious stories of his education as a vintner. His stories put her own anxieties in perspective. When the trip was over, Klaus invited her to a concert at Kloster Eberbach, an ancient monastery with extraordinary acoustics.

Again, Marielle had a wonderful time in his company, forgetting her loneliness and the stress of the business. He had a large extended family full of nieces and nephews, the children of his six brothers and sisters. Marielle felt herself absorbed with ease into Klaus's noisy and comfortable family. One summer evening she sat on his brother's veranda, watching the sunset as the adults enjoyed a bottle of

Klaus's Spätburgunder and the children played on the lawn.

It was a scene she hadn't expected to be a part of, and she was disturbed by prickles of dissatisfaction. She hadn't thought she wanted something as prosaic as this—a traditional vision of family life. It surprised her to be feeling this lack, and she went home that evening wondering if she would ever regret not marrying and having children.

She felt no physical attraction to Klaus, but she appreciated his humor and warmth. He became a friend, willing to coax her out of her driven focus on work. She even told him about Tomas.

All summer she questioned what might be missing from her life. She noticed women pushing strollers. When it was her turn to host the tasting stand at the village park she watched families walking, children on bikes, grandmothers doting on grandchildren. Was this a buried need that she had put aside? Would it haunt her? She didn't know the answer.

When Tomas came in October, he was thinner and more worn that she had ever seen him. Martial law had been imposed in the wake of strikes; civil liberties had been suspended and many union leaders had been imprisoned. His hospital had received many of the injured when government troops had attacked striking laborers. Once again, Poland had been in economic and political crisis. Marielle saw the human effect of the turmoil in Poland every time the crew arrived in the fall, but Tomas seemed to embody the ravages of failed policies more acutely than the others. When she took him into her bed the first night, she felt the unprotected angles of his body and sought to surround him with her own softness and comfort.

After a few weeks of work in the open air and Anita's hearty meals he had lost his gauntness. In his arms at night, Marielle felt his strength once again.

"Are you happy?" he asked her late one night after lovemaking.

"Yes. Being here with you is what makes my life meaningful."

"But is it enough? I look at you, how hard you work. And I see very little else, except waiting for these few weeks. You should be living, not waiting."

"When you are here, I forget the waiting."

"But when I'm not here…?"

He always seemed to be attuned to what she was thinking, despite her efforts to protect him this time from her doubts.

"Marielle, you're still a young woman, young enough to start a family. You're living half a life."

"I didn't think I needed the other half until…"

"Until what? Until someone?"

"Not someone in the way you mean. I'm not in love with someone else. But I was brought into a family this year, with children and grandparents and aunts and uncles, and I didn't know until I was in the midst of it that it represented a hole in my life."

"You could come to Poland and have that." His voice was pained. He knew she was not free to say yes, no matter how much she wanted that, wanted him.

She knew he wished that he could give her a whole life.

She still didn't know how to define that life.

They didn't resolve their dilemma that night. It hovered over them throughout the harvest and imbued their lovemaking with a desperation and hunger that drove them to a level of intensity that echoed their first time in Warsaw.

They exhausted themselves physically and emotionally. They talked in each other's arms, over the dinner table, on long walks on Sunday mornings along the river's edge.

As the Feast of St. Martin approached, Tomas came to a decision. He had seen the look on Marielle's face sometimes on Sunday when they passed families on the river path, a look she struggled to mask. But he knew her too well.

Like the centurion giving up his red cloak to the shivering beggar, Tomas gave up his claim to Marielle's heart.

"I need to set you free, Marielle. This is no life for you. Find what you need. Don't wake up twenty years from now full of regret and bitter that I couldn't let you go."

He left, as he always did, early the next morning. He kissed her for the last time and closed the gate to the courtyard behind him.

The rhythm of her life for the last eight years and the way she defined herself were disrupted, torn. For weeks, she went through the motions of running the winery and did nothing else. Klaus called to invite her to the Kiedricher Advent concert. He had been as busy as she with his own harvest, but had also kept his distance when Tomas was there. She accepted the invitation and was swept back up in Klaus's exuberant family. For a few months she entertained the idea of considering Klaus romantically, but when she couldn't imagine herself making love to him, she gently dissuaded him from the possibility that they could be a couple.

Gradually she opened herself up to meeting other men. Matchmaking friends of Anita's began to set up blind dates. She dutifully attempted to make conversation over dinners up and down the Rheingau. Now and then she went on a second date. For a while she became serious with a young scientist who shared her interest in rowing. She felt a "normalcy" in her social life.

But she missed Tomas more than she had expected. His empathy, his intensity, his tenderness, his understanding of who she was beneath the façade of a driven, smart businesswoman.

In the fall, Tomas returned for the harvest, but he did not work with Marielle. Instead, he joined a crew working another vineyard, the one where he had labored as a teenager. His path and Marielle's did not cross.

For four years, Marielle thought her desire for a family would override the reservations she had about one man or another. But she found that she could not will herself to love. Whenever she got close enough, she saw only what the men couldn't give her. In the winter of 1987, she received a proposal of marriage and turned it down. She spent the following spring and summer alone, deliberately withdrawing from the dating scene. She was in retreat from partnership and coupling.

During that time, she reread the hundreds of letters Tomas had written her over the years of their relationship. She sat up at night in bed, remembering and reliving.

She remembered as well his final conversation with her. "Don't look back with regret twenty years from now."

In October, after Janosch and the crew arrived, she

drove to the campground the first Sunday morning and knocked on the door of the camper. Tomas answered.

His hair was beginning to gray and the lines around his eyes had deepened. His hands, hanging at his sides, were still beautiful.

"I have no regrets," she said. "I want you in my life however and whenever you can be there."

She held her breath. She had no idea what had filled Tomas's life in the four years they had been apart. Had he found a woman who could be wife and mother in Poland?

He reached out his hand and stroked the side of her face, then gathered her into his arms, burying a moan in the hollow of her neck. She sobbed, her tears spilling onto his shoulder.

Chapter 12

November 1989

In 1989 when Tomas came back for the harvest, he once again moved into Marielle's apartment. In the evenings, instead of struggling to learn her craft as she had so many years before, Marielle painted. That fall, rather than her usual landscape, she painted Tomas's portrait.

She finished it at the beginning of November and had brought it to a shop in Wiesbaden to be framed. On November 9, she drove into the city to pick it up and take care of other errands. She was on her way back home and turned on the radio to catch the weather report.

The news was on, and the announcer's voice was

heightened, incredulous, jubilant. Marielle stopped her car and pulled over, not quite believing what she was hearing.

"Die Mauer ist weg!" The Berlin Wall had fallen.

Marielle was numb, disbelieving. She switched radio stations, thinking she had misheard or the reporter had made a mistake. But every station was reporting the same thing.

Trembling, she drove home, pulling the car into the courtyard and racing up the stairs to the apartment.

"Have you heard?' she burst into the apartment. Tomas, sitting in front of the television, nodded. He stood up and she ran to him, still trembling—because of what this meant for East and West Germany, for Eastern Europe, for them.

The months that followed were marked by hope, upheaval and a disruption of old ways and limited expectations. As welcome as the extraordinary change was in their lives and their definition of home, country, Europe, it was change nonetheless.

The patterns they had established, the rituals and boundaries that protected all of them, not just Tomas and Marielle, but those they loved—Magdalena, Halina, Nyanya, Anita—it all began to shift. Like a handful of loose rocks, skittering down the hillside, barely noticeable as they tumbled over closely cropped grass and carefully tended rows of vines. But the changes gathered momentum over the winter, like the muddy landslide set off by the heavy, unrelenting rains so long ago.

Marielle and Anita went to Warsaw for Christmas. Magdalena, twenty-one and in her second year of studies at Jagiellonian University, arrived home on the same day. Her hair, no longer in braids wrapped neatly around her head, was closely cropped and spiked, its little-girl blondness heightened to a near platinum shade. She wore American jeans and smoked French cigarettes and now used the name "Maggi." Nyanya chased her out to the balcony when she pulled out her cigarettes, scolding and complaining about what she had become.

At dinner on *Wigilia*, Christmas Eve, the Oplatek—the blessed bread—was passed from hand to hand, each of them taking a fragment as the first star appeared in the night sky.

"I have an announcement," Maggi held her vodka glass high, as if she was about to make a toast. I've been accepted to an exchange program at Juilliard in America; I start next September."

Everyone's glass went up in congratulations. Nyanya wiped her eyes with her napkin, her expression a mixture of pride in Magdalena's accomplishment combined with puzzlement and loss. Tomas looked at his daughter with eyes that revealed his surprise—not at her announcement, because she'd confided in him that she had applied to the conservatory. His surprise was his sudden recognition of Magdalena's confidence in her future, her embrace of the freedom she now had to define her life however she chose.

How had that fact escaped him? For so long he had been consumed with sheltering her, surrounding her with love to cushion her from the loss of her mother. That his love and protection could have formed her into a bird with such strong wings and even stronger desire to fly was a revelation to him that night.

It was the moment he realized that she had surpassed him, that she no longer needed him. And he was free.

On Christmas, a day of brilliant sunshine and biting cold, Tomas and Marielle walked home from church, their arms linked and their heads wrapped in wool scarves.

"I want to talk with you apart from the others," he said. "Stop with me a moment in the park."

They sat facing each other on a wooden bench that was free of snow.

"Magdalena's announcement last night cleared my head of a worry that I hadn't even known I was carrying. I think I finally saw her as a woman, eager to leap into this new world that's opening up for her generation. It made me feel old, but at the same time, I rejoiced for her." He looked away; his vulnerability palpable.

Marielle stroked the side of his check with her gloved hand and smiled.

"It also made me see that I have nothing to hold me back now, and it frightens me a little. I feel like an old woman who has become so used to limitations and confining restrictions that I cannot imagine any other kind of life. Until my daughter opened the door for me in a way the hole in the Berlin wall did not."

He placed his hand over Marielle's.

"Marry me, Marielle. Let me now give you the complete man. On your soil."

At dinner that afternoon they made their own announcement to the family and invited them all to the winery on Valentine's Day for the wedding.

In February, Maggi drove Halina and Nyanya across the boundaries that for so many years had been ominous barriers. Tomas had gone ahead, to begin looking for work and to start the paperwork to be licensed as a physician in Germany.

Marielle asked Maggi to be her maid of honor and took her shopping in Wiesbaen to find a dress that would both suit her nontraditional style and be something she would want to take to America in the fall. They spent an afternoon wandering in and out of small shops and department stores. As Maggi delighted in the selection of fabrics and the choices arrayed on the racks, Marielle watched her and saw not only herself at that age but the daughter she had never had.

Maggi's final choice was a black jersey wrap dress that was a striking counterpoint to her blondness and pale skin. Neither Halina nor Nyanya approved of its color or style—they would have preferred to see her as Magdalena, still in her traditional dirndl. But Marielle, about to become her mother, overruled their objections.

The villages of the Rheingau were preparing for Fasching, the German celebration of Carneval in the weeks leading up to Lent. Parades wound their way through the streets with floats full of costumed revelers tossing candy to children. Streamers and multicolored confetti flew through the air. It was a time of particular abandon in those first months of 1990, and Marielle and Tomas found themselves swept up in the music and the gaiety.

The morning of the wedding, Maria arrived with her usual delivery of Valentine roses, but instead of the dozen Tomas had always ordered in the past, he had requested ten times as many. Maria had combed the wholesale flower market in Frankfurt, corralling as many of the deep burgundy blooms as she could find.

The winery's public rooms were ablaze with color,

with bowls of roses on every table, set for the guests who would celebrate with them later in the day. Vases also rested on the windowsills formed by the meter-thick walls.

Rather than wear white, Marielle chose a dress the color of the roses, its velvet fabric echoing their texture. Her bouquet, in contrast, was white, with a single red rose in its center. She pinned another single rose to Tomas's lapel before they walked to the church.

During the wedding ceremony, Maggi played her violin for them, a vibrant and inventive rendition of "Spring" from Vivaldi's *Four Seasons*. Marielle felt the world coming to life for her and Tomas in those intense moments of music.

When they left the church on foot, followed by their guests, Maggi again put the violin to her chin and played as they strolled through the village to the winery. Along the way, friends opened windows and tossed confetti and streamers. By the time they arrived at the gate to the courtyard, Marielle's hair was entwined with the multicolored paper strands and Tomas's shoulders were covered with a dusting of confetti. At the reception they toasted each other and their guests with the 1988 Marcobruun, an extraordinary vintage that was to launch an incredible streak lasting eight years of great wines from the Rheingau.

Later that evening, as they lay in one another's arms for the first time as husband and wife, Tomas raised himself on one elbow and with his other hand traced circles on Marielle's belly.

"I've watched you in the last few days, taking on the role of Magdalena's mother as well as my wife, and I've thought how wonderful you are at it. A natural."

"Thank you." She kissed him.

"So I took that thought another step. What if we have a child now? You and I. You're only forty-one. I know you gave that up for me but, like everything else we thought we had forsaken—a life together, a future—we have a second chance. Why not?"

Marielle was still. A list of objections began to form in her mind, conditioned for so long not to want or imagine possible what she couldn't have.

But she knew that she had never completely abandoned her desire to have a child. For Tomas, with his daughter grown, to offer her this gift now overwhelmed her.

She burst into tears.

"Yes," she gulped, between the sobs.

Chapter 13

1991-2007

Valentin Marek was born a year later, on Valentine's Day, doubly blessing the day for them.

During the harvest of 1991, Valentin slept in a backpack borne alternately by his mother and father, the rhythm of their movements lulling him.

By the harvest of 1995, he followed after his great-uncle Janosch, dumping buckets of grapes into Janosch's carrier as the old man stooped to Valentin's height. By the harvest of 1998, Valentin had his own shears and worked the lower layers of the vines, only occasionally popping a handful of grapes into his mouth.

Maggi, when she finished her studies at Juilliard, won a seat with the Berlin Philharmonic. When her concert schedule allowed, she came back for the harvest, and she always made time in the summers to perform with Tomas in the courtyard concerts that had become signature events for the winery. In 2000 she made her first solo recording and Tomas and Marielle hosted a launch party for her at the winery.

By the time he was thirteen in 2004, Valentin was as tall as his father, with the same long fingers. He had inherited his mother's eyes and chestnut hair, which he wore in dreadlocks, much to Anita's dismay. He had also inherited Marielle's intensity, and was the winery's mechanic, fascinated by its equipment. He was less fascinated with school, and was chafing at the prospect of spending six more years preparing for the *Abitur* and then university, as his parents and his sister had before him.

On his sixteenth birthday he listened to the toasts of his parents and two grandmothers, made with wine from the case that had been set aside in his birth year. Each major event in his life—his baptism, his first day of school, his first communion—had been celebrated with the opening of a bottle from that case. On the occasion of his sixteenth birthday Marielle poured a small glass for him as well. After the toasts, Valentin stood, brushing back the hair from his eyes.

"I have a birthday wish," he said solemnly. "It's

something I've been thinking about for a while. I don't want to go to university."

He waited for the predictable objections, and his grandmothers did not disappoint. But Marielle and Tomas knew their son well enough to understand that something else was coming. They exchanged glances.

"I want to study winemaking instead. Maggi certainly isn't going to come back and take on the work, and who else but me?"

Marielle wanted to tell him it wasn't an expectation, that he was free to make his own way in life, even if that took him away from the land. But Tomas squeezed her hand and she let Valentin go on.

"If you'll agree, I can transfer to the wine institute in the fall. I'm not interested in spending years in a classroom like you two did. I'm much happier working with my hands—repairing the tractor, rigging the bottler, pruning and grafting the vines.

"I'm not like you, Papa; I don't have the patience to study for years and years. And Mama, I'll probably have to hire somebody to do the books when you've had enough of them. But I think I can make our hills flourish. What do you say?"

Marielle rose from the table and hugged him. Anita wiped her eyes. Even Halina was mollified.

Later that night, Tomas and Marielle took a walk. The

moon was full, and sharing their anniversary with their son's birthday had led them to take time for themselves at the end of the day. The night was cold but clear and they headed up the vineyard path to the top of the hill.

Tomas kissed her, taking her face in his hands.

"You've raised quite a young man, Mrs. Marek."

"So have you, Dr. Marek."

"No disappointments?"

"None. He's much surer of himself than I was at his age."

Tomas nodded. "And much happier than I was."

"Are you happy now, Tomas?"

"Happier than I have ever been."

Acknowledgments

I am so grateful to my friend Ursula von Breitenbach, who not only taught me how to harvest grapes and judge a fine Riesling vintage, but also renewed my creative spirit with long weekends devoted to painting and poetry (and more Riesling). My special thanks also to Kasia Novak, whose memories of childhood summers in Warsaw added vibrancy and richness to my research.

A special note of thanks to Christine Richardson, my Bellastoria Press assistant, for her curiosity, skill and creativity in designing and formatting, and for her warmth and support as we brought this book to its completion.

To the friends and family who supported me in my earliest years as an author, I also offer a warm thank you—especially to Betsy Port, who cheered me on with infectious enthusiasm; Lani Kretschmar, who listened to my daily musings and plottings and lent her keen eye to proofreading; Toni Robinson, who spread the word far and wide to her network; and to my sister, Cindy McLaughlin, and my cousins Joan Cito, Mari Adele Thomas and Gene Vetrano, who were my "street team."

Linda Cardillo is an award-winning author of historical fiction and historical romance. She writes about the old country and the new, the tangle and embrace of family, and finding courage in the midst of loss.

She is also co-founder of Bellastoria Press, an independent publisher of compelling and beautiful stories.

In an earlier life Linda worked as an editor of college textbooks before earning an MBA at Harvard Business School at a time when women represented only 15% of the class. Armed with her Harvard degree, she managed the circulation of *Inc.* magazine during its successful start- up, founded a catering business and then built a career as the author of several works of nonfiction, from from articles in *The New York Times* to books on marketing and corporate policy. Throughout her professional life and while raising her family, she nurtured her intention to write fiction. Her debut novel, *Dancing on Sunday Afternoons*, which launched Harlequin's Everlasting Love series, was published in 2007.

When she isn't writing, Linda loves to cook and is happiest when the twelve chairs around her dining room table are filled with people enjoying her food. She speaks four languages, some better than others. She plays the piano every night—sometimes by herself and sometimes in an improvisational duet with her younger son. She does *The New York Times* Sunday crossword puzzle in ink, a practice she learned from her mother. From her mother she also absorbed a love of opera, especially those of Puccini and Verdi, whose music filled her home when she was a child. She once climbed Mt. Kenya and has very curly hair.

For news and upcoming events, previews of new work, and musings on the writing life, sign up for Linda's newsletter at lindacardillo.com.